D1384778

The THIEF of HEARTS

Mary Blount Christian

Annie's®
AnniesFiction.com

The Thief of Hearts
Copyright © 2016 Annie's.

Library of Congress-in-Publication Data
The Thief of Hearts / by Mary Blount Christian
p. cm.
I. Title
                    2016939192

AnniesFiction.com
(800) 282-6643
Secrets of the Quilt™
Series Creator: Shari Lohner
Series Editors: Shari Lohner, Janice Tate, and Ken Tate
Cover Illustrator: Jonathan Bouw

10 11 12 13 14 | Printed in China | 9 8 7 6 5 4 3 2 1

1

Cabot Falls, Vermont
Present Day

Sofia Parker looked up as her husband, Jim, strode into the kitchen, stretching out the kinks he'd collected from his night in the backyard tent. She poured him a cup of coffee and offered him a muffin fresh from the oven. "So how was the campout? The boys awake?"

Jim kissed her. "Good morning. They're still sleeping. We lost Matthew during the night. Did roughing it lose its glamour?"

Sofia laughed. "He slipped in about two this morning. He said his bed was lonesome."

"Wise beyond his years," Jim said. He bit into the muffin. "Mmm, my favorite—fruit and nuts. What more can a man ask for?"

"An omelet?" Sofia replied. "So how is Bryce doing?" Her fourteen-year-old nephew was spending part of the summer with them while her sister Gina McCray helped her husband, Jack, campaign for reelection to his senate seat in Massachusetts.

"He's loosening up a little," Jim said. "It takes quality time with our rough-and-tumble boys to break through that cautious formality he developed at prep school. Bryce is a good kid, but it has to be tough to be under media scrutiny all the time. It's like they just hang around, hoping for a misstep."

"Well, nobody in Vermont is spying on him," Sofia said, breaking two eggs into a bowl and whisking them as she spoke.

"So what did you do last night while I braved raccoons, owls, and snoring kids?" Jim licked a muffin crumb off his lip. "Mmm."

"I started research on another quilt square, that pretty silvery-pink one with embroidery. The diary didn't give much detail, just *Chicago 1871* and *Pinkerton*. It had a question mark by the name Hannah Reed. The date sounded familiar, so I looked it up. It's the year of the famous Chicago fire."

Jim set down his coffee cup. "Pinkerton, you say? Isn't that the famous detective agency? It would be interesting to have another detective in the family tree."

Sofia raised an eyebrow. "*Another* detective? But who?"

"You, sweetheart! You're detecting every time you uncover another clue to your family heirloom."

"I guess I never thought of it that way," Sofia said.

Her late grandmother, Elena Baresi—known as Nonna to her family—had named her steward of the unique quilt of blocks from women whose lives had spanned more than five centuries. Sofia wanted to learn as much as she could about her ancestors.

The whine of electric saws cut through the quiet as Sofia retrieved mushrooms and grated cheese from the fridge. "Those renovations next door are taking forever."

"Sofia, don't tell me you're anxious to have him move in. Jessop Norton keeps the neighborhood in an uproar, and he hasn't even moved in yet," Jim reminded her.

"Maybe I should take over some muffins next time he's over there."

"I'm afraid it's going to take more than your delicious muffins to penetrate that harsh exterior."

Sofia slid the omelet plate toward Jim. "That man is disgusting! He is so disagreeable. First he got a cease-and-desist order to keep the kids from building a tree house in their own yard. Then he called the police to stop Matthew from setting up a lemonade stand. Who wants to stop a ten-year-old kid from having a lemonade stand? It's an American tradition."

Jim shrugged. "And don't forget that he stopped Luke and me from building birdhouses in the workshop. He called it 'operating a business in a zoned neighborhood.' He even called the police with a 'loose dog' complaint on Pat's little poodle. Willow never leaves her side, even without a leash. He's a miserable man, and he won't be happy until he's made all of us miserable."

"He's certainly abusing his office as alderman," Sofia said. "I just hate to think that he'll be living next—"

The phone rang. When Sofia answered, she was startled to hear the voice of Samuel Goodson. "Mr. Mayor!"

"Sofia, as you know, the Founder's Day Celebration is coming up next month."

"Yes, the Pinot Painters signed up for a face-painting booth. That's always popular at events like that."

"Great. I want this to be the biggest and best one ever. That brings me to the reason for my call. We need to show all our visitors that we are a great place to live. I want every shop on the square open for business. I guess you read that the Drummonds retired to Florida."

"Yes, and I see that the Andersons bought them out and will turn it into a soup-and-salad place."

"That's my problem. They can't open their business until the fall. That leaves a boarded-up shop on the square during Founder's Day. That's unacceptable."

"Sam, I see how that isn't the image you want to put forth, but—"

"Angie reminded me of what a super job you did catering our daughter's wedding. She suggested that you set up a sweetshop," the mayor said.

"Oh, I don't know, Sam. I've already committed to a third of the painting booth fee. I can't—"

"That's the beauty of this, Sofia. The Andersons said as long as I get a responsible person who'll guarantee to return the place to its original state, it's rent free. It'll be a great chance to introduce your catering to anyone who doesn't already know. Plus it'd be a huge favor to me and to our fair town. Besides, I'm not looking forward to rolling a lemon down the sidewalk of Grand Point with my nose."

She burst out laughing. "Don't tell me you made another bet with your old college roomie, Sam." Sam and Daryl Pines, the mayor of Grand Point, had been good-natured competitors ever since they met in college. The neighboring villages were about the same population and had been founded about the same time in the early eighteenth century by brothers, so that rivalry was the natural result.

Sam laughed. "What else could I do? I don't mind a little humiliation for myself. But the reputation of Cabot Falls is at stake here. Tell me you'll do it. Please?"

"I'll have to think about it. I promise to let you know tomorrow afternoon, if that's okay. Give Angie my best." She hung up. "Well, that was certainly interesting."

"What's that?" Jim asked.

She poured them second cups of coffee while she repeated the conversation. "But that would leave the Pinot Painters short-handed, and I've already paid my third of the fee."

"Vanessa and Wynter are both good at face painting, and they'd have a blast doing it too. Sam's right about one thing. It would be a good chance to expand your client list. Let's look at the shop and make sure that it's doable. What about insurance, just in case the unexpected happens?"

"I didn't even think to ask." Sofia didn't want to let her hometown down, even if the image of Sam rolling a lemon with his nose was intriguing. Angie had sent a lot of business her way, and it would be beneficial to publicize her catering.

Before she could say yes, she needed to consult with her partners in the painting booth, her fellow Pinot Painters, Julie Butler and Marla Dixon. They were best friends, and they met once a week to paint, chat, and enjoy a glass of their namesake wine while tasting Sofia's latest baked treat. Today she had baked two lemon loaves, one for the painters and the other for Jim and the kids, who promised to eat and then go to the movies.

When her friends arrived, she explained Sam's proposal. "Would I be terrible if I did that instead of working in the painting booth? I won't unless you agree."

"It's a wonderful idea," Marla said. "The girls would be great helpers. And it seems like a win-win situation for you and the mayor."

"One little caveat," Julie added. "Let us help you get the shop ready, and we get all we can eat, especially if you offer lemon loaf. This is melt-in-your-mouth delicious!"

Later, when Sofia asked Vanessa and Wynter for their help, they eagerly agreed to be in the painting booth. Meanwhile, Sofia called Sam to ask about a temporary business permit and who would be responsible for short-term insurance for the shop. Sam called back later to say he had requested that the town council purchase temporary insurance to cover two weeks, including the preparation time before the big day. "It was nearly unanimous," Sam said.

"You don't have to tell me the negative vote. It was my new neighbor, Jessop Norton. That man is fast becoming the bane of my existence."

"I have to work with him," Sam said. "I'd sure hate to have to live next door to him. I don't know why he wanted to be an alderman. He hasn't voted yea since he was elected. You can pick up the keys to the shop anytime, Sofia. Mark Keeler has them down at the real estate office. You are going to do it, right?"

Sofia laughed. "You drive a hard bargain, Sam. I'm in."

Sofia realized that it would be tough to get ready in time. Fortunately, she had a backlog of basic cakes in the freezer. It would give her a head start on baked goods.

Jim settled the boys in the basement with video games, and the girls retired to their room to work on face designs. Sofia boxed two German chocolate cakes, a white cake with pineapple filling, and two shoofly pies. The Cabot Inn was expecting the desserts for the dinner crowd. The check would help pay for the ingredients, paper plates, and forks for Founder's Day.

Leaving Jim in the car, she delivered her goods at the rear door of the inn's kitchen and then cut through the dining area to the lobby. Even before she saw the commotion, she recognized that voice. It was Norton. He was living at the inn while his home was being readied for occupancy.

"My bedsheets are scratchy. The pillow is too hard. The drapes need to be vacuumed or replaced. I sneezed, and I do not have allergies or a cold. There's an odor in my room," he complained loudly. "I insist on a new mattress. My bed is lumpy, and I can't sleep. As alderman, I could shut this place down, you know." He stalked off and punched the call button for the elevator.

Sofia waited until the elevator doors closed before she approached the desk. "What's with the princess and the pea?"

The clerk laughed. "Thanks for that. He's driving all of us crazy. I can hardly wait until he moves out." She handed Sofia an envelope with her check.

"You wouldn't say that if he was moving next door to you," Sofia replied. "He has the whole neighborhood stirred up."

"He wouldn't have been elected alderman if he'd had an opponent. You should run against him next time," the clerk said. "I have the slogan: A cake on every plate."

Waving her off, Sofia retraced her steps to her Suburban. She wanted to grab the keys from the real estate agent and go with Jim to look the shop over. She just hoped there wasn't a lot of work to do. She needed to bake.

Sofia soon parked at the south end of the row of shops. "It's the one with the paper covering the window," she told Jim. "Sam said the electricity is already on. So is the gas."

Inside, Jim took photos and measurements of the outer room and the kitchen. "I think if we use those removable Velcro tabs, we could hang butcher paper to cover the walls. That way, you can decorate however you want and we won't have to repaint when it's over."

"Great idea," Sofia said. "I've seen all I need to. Marla and Julie will paint some Old World decorations. What if I call it *La Dolce Vita*?"

"'The sweet life.' I like that." Jim turned out the lights and closed the door behind them.

Sofia locked the door. As she turned to leave, she found herself face-to-face with her soon-to-be neighbor. "You!" he exclaimed. He muttered something she didn't understand and then added, "Isn't it enough that you and your motley crew are next door to my home? Now you're here too?"

Sofia's cheeks grew warm. *Motley crew?* If she'd had any idea that he had a shop next door, she never would have agreed to this project. She turned on her heel and stalked to the car before she said something she'd regret. She had the distinct feeling that this was the harbinger of more trouble for the Parker family.

2

Chicago, Illinois
Summer 1867

The door shut behind Hannah with an emphatic click. She had heard that latch many times over the last eighteen years. But this time, she was on the stoop outside, shut out from its emotionally cold but protected environment. Suddenly blinded by the tears that she promised would not come, she murmured, "What do I do now? Where am I supposed to go?"

Her plain gray gingham dress defined her to Chicagoans as surely as the scarlet *A* defined Hester Prynne in Hawthorne's novel: She was unwanted, unloved even by the mother who gave life to her—a "graduate" of Whiteside Orphanage. Hannah knew in her heart that neither she nor Hester Prynne should be defined by a single event. But would anyone look beyond the telltale clothes that said she was a throwaway child?

Her mother hadn't wanted her. And now the orphanage didn't want her. The proprietor's words echoed in her head: "You're eighteen and no longer a ward of the state. I need to make room for a child I get paid for." Greta had shrugged helplessly. "But you're smart, and you're resourceful, Hannah. You'll be fine."

Hannah fingered the smooth round top button of her dress. She knew that the younger girls were pressed against the window, watching. She had to appear strong for them. Wiping away her tears, she turned and smiled at them, waving. Who would tell them bedtime stories now? Who would teach them to dream of better things? After the girls were ushered away from the window, Hannah plopped down on the stoop in dismay.

Where was Betsy? Betsy Day had aged out of the orphanage the previous April. She had stood on this very stoop. "Hannah," she had said, "I will come for you on your birthday. You can stay with me, and I'll help you adjust. I promise."

But the sidewalk was empty of pedestrians. Hannah balled her fists, wondering how many times she must endure abandonment.

She squared her shoulders. Her tall, slender figure cast a thin shadow on the walkway. She picked up the reed basket Greta had handed her as she'd escorted her out. "You had these when you came here," Greta said. It was the first time Hannah had seen the items.

That basket was how she came to have the last name Reed. Greta had named her Hannah because *H* is the eighth letter of the alphabet, and she had arrived during August, the eighth month in the year. But Greta had never mentioned the basket's contents before. *Why not?*

Numb from the brusque dismissal, Hannah had accepted the basket and the dollar in coins tied in a handkerchief. "Be careful, Hannah." That had been Greta's parting advice.

Unsure what to do next, she walked to the church where she and the other girls, like ducklings in their dull, gray uniforms, had marched behind Greta to fill a pew near the altar. Hannah entered the vestibule where sunlight coming in through stained glass windows stretched colorfully across the worn oak floor. She pulled open the heavy carved door to the sanctuary, and the aroma of burning tallow assaulted her senses.

Along the walls, woeful-looking saints and images of the seven stations of the cross seemed to stare at her. Out of habit, she took a seat in the pew the wards occupied every Sunday and began examining the basket. How small she must have been to fit in it. How could anyone abandon such a small, helpless infant?

She picked up the silk baby quilt, rubbing it against her cheek. It was soft and comforting. *It must be filled with the finest goose down,* she thought. The silk, in contrast to her faded, coarse cotton dress, looked expensive. The pale pink reminded her of a rosebud.

The hand-stitching was even and neat. Someone had taken special care to create the quilt. So why had it been wrapped around her, an unwanted infant? She noticed a bit of embroidery at one corner: *A.J.* Could they be her true initials? Annie? Abigail? Appoline? And J—had she been born a Jasper or a Jenkins, perhaps? Along the hem was a jumble of letters: *a ghrá mo chroí.*

Something in the basket reflected the flicker of candle flames. It was a gold locket. She opened it and sucked in her breath, letting it out slowly as she stared at the image. She recognized it. She had seen that face; it looked back at her from the mirror every day. The young woman in the locket held a steady gaze. She had the same button nose, same full lips, same high cheekbones. Her hair looked dark. Hannah wondered if it was deep mahogany like hers. And she was wearing the very locket Hannah now held in her fingers.

Hannah felt warm tears spill onto her cheeks. "Mother, who are you? Where are you? Why didn't you want me?" Until this very moment, Hannah had denied that she wanted to know about her birth family. Now, staring into her mother's eyes, the need burned into her very soul. What if inside her was that same cold heart that could leave a helpless baby on the steps of a church? Dare she even dream of having a family of her own?

"I will find you," Hannah said to the fading photo. "But first, I will become someone to respect, someone worthy of the love you denied me."

Hannah put the necklace on and slipped it inside her dress. It had hung around her mother's neck too. It and the quilt were the only links to her hidden past, the only clues about her identity.

She carefully refolded the quilt. None of this helped her right now. She needed a place to sleep and food to eat. Hannah knew little of the things outside the orphanage, but she felt sure that the dollar would not last long. Who would hire her in an orphanage uniform?

An uneasy weariness overwhelmed Hannah, and her shoulders sagged. Nearly every day she had slipped into Greta's elegant private parlor to read the newspaper about the Pinkerton detectives. Each article read like an episode in an exciting novel. She drew courage from reading about the woman they called the Chameleon—proof that women could do anything, given the opportunity. *If she can, I can*, Hannah thought often.

She had risked punishment by slipping away with Greta's books to read them. But she was not to be denied the best education she could sneak. Hannah had believed that she would be ready for the outside world—until now, that is. She closed her eyes.

"Hannah?"

She jumped at the touch on her shoulder. "Father!"

The priest raised an eyebrow. "You've been sitting there a long time, Hannah. Won't Greta be concerned about your absence?"

"I am no longer Greta's concern, Father Joshua. I have reached my majority and can no longer live at Whiteside Orphanage. I must have dozed off. I am so sorry. May I stay awhile longer?"

"Hannah, I'm sorry, but you must leave. I must lock the outer doors. The gangs come at night and rob the poor box and deface the icons. I don't like shutting out good folks, but as steward, I'm left little choice."

"I—I don't know where to go, Father. This is all so new to me."

Father Joshua sighed. "I suppose it will be all right if you remain here just this one night. But first thing tomorrow, you must find other arrangements."

"Thank you, Father. I promise to leave as soon as you reopen the doors." Satisfied that she was safe, Hannah lay on the bench with her head on the folded quilt. How long had she rested on it as an infant, she wondered, before she was left on the stone steps of the orphanage?

Several times in the night, she awoke, confused as to where she was. Some of the prayer candles had gone out, and it was dimmer now so that the statues looked eerily unfamiliar in the flickering light that bounced off their glazed faces. The hard bench pressed into her body, and she missed the sounds of the other girls' breathing.

Why hasn't Betsy come? Has she forgotten her promise? A terrifying thought intruded. *Has something bad happened to Betsy?*

Did the same fate wait for her?

The next morning, Hannah left as promised. Her stomach growled, and the thought of the oatmeal mush at the orphanage seemed much more inviting than it had the previous morning. She walked south and found herself suddenly amidst the hubbub of commerce. There were horse-drawn carriages and trams with drivers shouting at one another, horseback riders, and pedestrians everywhere. Elegantly dressed people hurried past her without a glance. The women looked so fine in their jaunty plumed hats, and the men looked like newspaper ads come to life in full color.

The smell of coffee called her attention to the café. She squared her shoulders and walked in with an air of confidence she didn't feel. Hannah sat at a small table by the window. An older woman, wearing a stiff, white apron that covered most of her dark cotton dress, handed her a list of food and drinks.

Dismayed, Hannah could see her meager coins quickly vanishing. "A cup of coffee and one biscuit," she told the server.

Hannah saw a newspaper on one of the chairs and retrieved it. She turned to the advertisements as the server brought her order. She ate slowly, pausing to read the ads between bites. She was startled as the chair across the table scraped the floor and a nattily dressed man asked, "May I?"

Hannah scowled suspiciously. "There are unoccupied tables."

"Yes, but they don't have you at them." He smiled, revealing a crown on one canine tooth that was as gold and shiny as the locket she wore. His dark hair was oiled and as shiny as patent leather, and it matched his mustache. He wore a diamond stickpin in his tie. It caught the sunlight and reflected on the wall like a prism. Ignoring her suggestion, he sat down and leaned his cane against the table. The carved snake head had shiny red eyes.

Hannah stared at it, mesmerized. *Why would anyone want such a hideous cane?* she wondered.

He plunked his top hat over it. "So you were cast from the orphanage like yesterday's news," he said. "That meager meal will not sustain you in a search for a job, young lady." He snapped his fingers without looking and said, "Bring this lady your special with eggs, sausage, and another biscuit—my treat."

"No! I can't accept it," Hannah protested. She waved off the waitress. This stranger knew far too much about her. She promised herself that her first purchase when she got a job would be a replacement for this telltale dress.

Undaunted, the man continued. "Without a job, the meager little stipend Greta sent you off with will get you only a few nights at a boarding establishment."

He knew Greta? Even how much money she had? Hannah felt a flash of anger that this stranger knew so much and she knew nothing of him.

"Allow me to introduce myself. I am Carlton Vanhiller, Esquire. My dear wife and I take in some of you young ladies now and then, and we give you job training, room, and board. I have a soft spot for orphans, being one myself." He smiled, flashing his gold tooth again.

Her stomach growled, and she regretted rejecting his offer of a meal. "Did you take in a ward named Betsy Day?" she asked.

His mustache shifted as he momentarily tightened his lips in a straight line. He seemed to quickly recover and smiled. "Betsy Day. Hmm. I do seem to recall a young girl by that name a year or so ago. She moved on after our hospitality, though. Went east, I believe. Maybe New York City."

Hannah wondered why Betsy had not written to her if she was leaving Chicago. It was thoughtless—unlike her. She wondered if he really knew Betsy or if he had said that to put her at ease. Hannah stood, shoving her chair back abruptly. "I'm leaving, Mr. Vanhiller. Please, stay and enjoy your meal."

He stood. "My card, my dear." He flipped it on top of the quilt as she grabbed her basket. "You may find the outside more difficult than you think. My offer is open-ended."

She grabbed the newspaper and stepped out onto the busy sidewalk.

Relieved when the man did not follow her, Hannah spent the day applying for any kind of job she could, from ribbon girl to laundress, from seamstress to dishwasher. When businesses closed for the day, she was still left with no job and no place to stay. As dusk closed in, she felt the city closing in on her too. She imagined every pedestrian as a predator. The gaslights flickered on, bathing the streets in a soft glow and casting foreboding shadows that seemed to reach out for her.

The streets cleared, and the click of her heels on the sidewalk seemed magnified as they echoed off windows. A commotion at the end of the block summoned her attention. She saw ten, perhaps a dozen silhouettes of rowdies with sticks, and they were coming her way, shouting and hooting. One hurled a rock; a window shattered. Hannah slipped into an arched doorway and pressed herself into the shadows until they passed. Her heart beat so hard that she feared they might hear it.

She heard the clatter of hooves on the cobblestone street. It was a carriage for hire. Terrified, Hannah rushed to the curb and hailed the driver. She shoved Vanhiller's card into his hand. "Is this far?"

The driver tipped his hat. "Miss, you shouldn't be out here like this. It isn't safe, but me and Tulip here are done for the day. We're heading to the stable."

"Oh, please! I can pay!" Hannah handed him her coins.

He sighed heavily and handed them back to her. "Don't worry about that, miss. Come on. I guess Tulip is good for one more jaunt today."

It was Hannah's first ride in a carriage, and she might have relished it more had she not been so apprehensive. The driver passed the lighted areas and turned onto a dark residential street with two-story homes that were shuttered or draped so there was little light. He stopped in front of an imposing mansion surrounded by an iron fence that reminded Hannah of a line of spears. The yard beyond was bare of shrub or grass.

"This is it, miss. Are you sure this is where you want to go?"

Hannah leaned forward, straining to see details of the structure. The windows were covered with iron bars, and not only the ground floor but also the top. Considering Vanhiller, she had expected something showier. Nothing was outstanding or memorable about the place. All of the shades were drawn. The light inside made them appear like melted butter, even less inviting than the orphanage.

Unease took the guise of goose bumps that crept up Hannah's spine and wrapped icy fingers around her neck, making it hard to swallow. She let her breath out in resignation.

"Miss?" The driver's voice sounded edgy. "Are you going to get out or not?"

Hesitantly, Hannah stepped down with her basket. Her legs were stiff as she stepped onto the stoop and twisted the bell knob. Greta's words echoed in her head: "Be careful, Hannah."

What choice did she have? It was too dangerous to remain unescorted in the city. And this was only until she found a job. *Be careful, Hannah!*

She squared her shoulders as she heard a key turning in the lock. The door opened, and she stood face to face with a dark-haired woman with soulful eyes and thin lips. Wordlessly, the woman stepped aside and motioned for Hannah to enter.

Once inside, Hannah turned in time to see the woman lock and bolt the door and slip the key into her skirt pocket. It was as if an alarm sounded in her mind. Stunned momentarily, she stood, staring wordlessly.

What have I gotten myself into?

3

Cabot Falls, Vermont
Present Day

"What have I gotten myself into?" Sofia moaned. Running a shop for even one day took a lot of effort. She had been delighted when Marla called to say she had enough free butcher paper to cover the shop walls. Jim secured the panels with Velcro tabs, and the Pinot Painters set to work giving them a warm Tuscan gold in washable, quick-drying paint. Sofia, with Vanessa and Wynter, added details of grapevines and rambling roses. When the girls finished, they took their lunches and went across to the town square to watch the booth construction around its perimeter. Volunteers already had draped red, white, and blue banners around the bandstand.

Adding to the confusion of hammers and saws was a cacophony of tubas, trumpets, and drums; the high school band remained together during vacation to participate.

When Jim tested the appliances in the shop, he found a bad breaker and a plumbing leak under the sink. The city health inspector would have to approve the repairs before they could open for business. Not even the mayor's influence was going to make that man move a minute sooner than he wanted.

So he'd have access to the electric control panel, Sofia created a paper flap painted to resemble a pair of shutters. That done, they spread a picnic cloth on the floor, and Sofia handed out turkey-and-provolone-cheese sandwiches with sweet-potato chips and peach iced tea. She had baked saucer-size chocolate chip cookies for dessert.

Marla unwrapped her sandwich before she asked, "Have you had any luck finding Hannah Reed, Sofia?"

"Not a lot," Sofia said. "I think the big fire of 1871 destroyed a lot of records. Maybe that's why there is a question mark by her name in the diary. I found a genealogy website that shows an H. Reed living at Whiteside Orphanage in Chicago in 1865. The age seems right. Right now, she's a big mystery. Notations in the diary mention a Z. Benetti in Vermont too. But none of those names explain the initials A.J. on the quilt square. The information is as much a patchwork as the quilt itself."

Marla set her tea down. "I'm running into the same problems trying to do the history of Cabot Falls for the Founder's Day program. There's only one Cabot kin left, although I can't find where he is now. As far as I can figure out, the Cabot Falls Inn is still owned by the family estate. The first little courthouse and all the records burned during the war, so I'm spending a lot of time going through old church records; nothing is computerized. Everywhere I look, I'm told, 'Now we don't need to mention that' or 'That has nothing to do with the founding of our village.' But I think it's the people and how they react to their challenges that are interesting. Dates and names are boring."

Julie laughed. "Rattling a few skeletons in the closet will make it much more interesting, Marla. After all, whatever it is, it's in the past; how can it hurt anyone now? My own family history is so boring. I'd love to find an ancestor with a bit of mystery about her."

Sofia crumpled the sandwich wrapper and stuck it inside her empty paper cup. "Church records are a great idea, Marla. If I can find a Chicago map from that era, I'll check for schools and churches near the orphanage. They probably attended the nearest one."

Jim, who had been replacing the leaky gooseneck pipe under the sink, joined them. He retrieved a sandwich from the basket.

Marla poured tea into a paper cup and handed it to him. "Are you enjoying being a volunteer firefighter this summer, Jim?"

"We've sure been busy lately—almost every night. Vacant buildings and stolen cars so far, but the investigator is sure it's arson. The police said it may be only a matter of time before the firebug escalates to residences."

"That's troubling news, Jim," Julie said. "They don't have any leads?"

"Not that I've heard. The mayor was on TV last night to announce a reward for information," Jim replied. "The council had to tap into the disaster funds to get us more fire-retardant foam. We are already running out of what is usually a year's supply."

"I heard that," Marla said. "The mayor suggested that we check our fire alarm batteries and report anything suspicious. I never thought that big-city crime would come to our quiet little village."

"You all could put out a firefighter calendar to raise money," Julie teased. "I hear that they are really popular. I'd buy one."

"I think that's my cue to call the inspector again," Jim said. "I need to see if we have to do anything else to be legal." He turned toward Sofia with a "help me out here" look.

She shrugged helplessly and joined in the laughter. She took his wrapper and cup and stuffed it into the trash bag with the others. "Anyone else want this last sandwich?" she asked.

"No, but I'll take one of those chocolate chip cookies," Marla said.

When no one wanted seconds, Sofia said, "I'm going to take these leftovers next door, then."

Julie gasped. "To that grouchy Jessop Norton? Not even your

delicious food will melt that man's heart. You're only asking to be insulted again."

"I know," Sofia admitted. "I just have to try." Although the sandwich and cookie were already wrapped in cellophane, she wrapped them together in a red-checked paper napkin and poured the remainder of the tea and ice into a mason jar.

The door to Norton's shop was open, so Sofia walked in. Norton stood between two large men, and when he looked up, Sofia thought he had that deer-in-the-headlights look. The conversation stopped midsentence.

"You ever heard of knocking?" the larger of the two snapped. His hair was cropped short, like the recent growth from a prison buzz cut, and his expression was pure fury.

Startled, Sofia jammed the food into Norton's hands, muttered an apology, and hastily retreated. She reentered her shop, puzzling over what she had just witnessed.

"Sofia? Are you all right?" Marla asked. "You look as if you just witnessed a train wreck."

"Maybe I did, in a way." She couldn't exactly explain why, but she had the odd sensation that something was very wrong.

Chicago, Illinois
Summer 1867

Hannah stood in the entry hall, face-to-face with the woman who held the key to her escape in her pocket. Neither spoke a word. Had she seen in the woman's eyes a flicker of regret? If so, it quickly was replaced by a visage of fear, or perhaps it was anxiety.

The woman's clothes were plain and worn. Her gray-streaked ebony hair was drawn into a bun; stray tendrils hung limply. She wore no jewelry except for a thin gold band on her ring finger.

The hall was eerily quiet so that the only sounds Hannah heard were her own quick breaths and approaching footsteps. She turned to face Vanhiller, who had lured her here with his offer to help.

Hannah was no stranger to defending herself. One could not live with a dozen semicaged females of varying ages without a scuffle or two over the years. Personal space was a precious commodity well worth fighting for.

But here she was outnumbered. Vanhiller was a small man, but his vicious cane more than compensated for his lack of size.

She pretended she hadn't noticed that she was trapped. Perhaps they eventually would let down their guard. With no clues to her true identity, she had entertained herself pretending that she was a famous actress, a runaway princess, and a famous novelist. Pretending to be a clueless victim barely stretched reality. She turned toward Vanhiller and forced a smile.

"Ah, my dear, you decided to take me up on my offer," Vanhiller said. His words slipped from his mouth as though greased with butter. "You must be hungry, yes?" He looked past her at the woman. "Millie, did you keep supper warm on the stove for our guest as I asked?" His manner was as oily as his hair.

Wordlessly, the woman skittered around both of them and disappeared behind a door at the end of the hall.

Hannah wondered if Vanhiller really had been so sure that she'd come. How many times had he done the same thing for other unsuspecting women? Had Betsy been attracted by the thought of safety as she had? How many "graduates" from Whiteside had he sweet-talked to this lair? Did Greta know?

As she followed him toward the closed door, she passed several open ones. On her right was a parlor much like Greta's at the orphanage. With a hurricane oil lamp and a single comfortable reading chair, it spoke of solitude. Although it was early evening, there was no sign of other occupants—no chatting, no creak of floorboards upstairs.

To her left, she saw a room devoid of furniture except for a wooden park bench. At first she thought she saw people standing rigidly in the dark, but it was a cluster of mannequins. In the dim light, their silhouettes looked ominous, as if they were frozen in time like the icons at church.

She tried to guess what the Vanhillers needed with all those mannequins. Perhaps they trained the women as tailors and seamstresses. But where were the worktables? Hannah nodded as Vanhiller opened the kitchen door and motioned for her to enter. The kitchen was spacious, with a woodburning stove and an icebox, its drip pan beneath nearly full. The dinner table beckoned, so she selected a chair.

Millie hastily brought milk and a plate of fragrant stew to the painted table and wiped the fork with the hem of her apron before setting it down next to the plate. It was all Hannah could do to keep from gobbling the food.

Vanhiller's eyes narrowed as he watched her devour the stew, sopping the juice with a thick slice of homemade bread.

Hannah drank the milk, not setting the glass down until she had drained it. "Thank you, ma'am. That was delicious."

Millie nodded before snatching the plate and glass and rushing to the sink to wash them. So far, she had not uttered even a whimper. Hannah wondered if Millie was mute or if she was afraid to speak.

Hannah smiled. "I'm so anxious to meet my fellow trainees." She watched his face for any hint about his feelings, but he gave none.

"In time, my dear," Vanhiller said. "In time."

The outside door opened, and a large man plodded in with a waste bin. Although he wore a suit that seemed to be in the current style, it was ill fitting and showed signs of neglect, such as the simple brushing away of mud splatter. His posture was slouched and almost apologetic. At first Hannah thought perhaps she had met him before. Then she realized that his features were an older, more-damaged version of Vanhiller. He moved about clumsily and with effort. "I took care of it, Carl."

"Very good, Lucas." Vanhiller's tone was almost solicitous. "My brother," he told Hannah. His voice was uncharacteristically tender when he spoke of the man.

She sensed in Vanhiller a genuine respect for the awkward man. Had she misjudged the situation? Perhaps Vanhiller and his wife were truly benevolent.

"Why don't you empty the drip pan and then retire for the evening, Lucas?" Vanhiller's voice was tender, as if he were speaking to a child.

"Yes. Thank you," Lucas mumbled.

Hannah saw that one of Lucas's ears was distorted with lumps and knots, much like the florets of a cauliflower. She knew she must have been staring, because he suddenly put his hand over it and turned away, lumbering off to another room.

Hannah flushed with embarrassment. "I—I shouldn't have stared. That was so rude of me."

"An old . . . accident . . . when we were children. It was a long time ago." Vanhiller's eyes darkened, and he seemed momentarily to lose his suave manners. His head jerked, and he shoved back his chair. "I'll show you to your room. Tomorrow we'll discard that uniform and get you some proper clothes."

The thought of shedding the hideous gray checked uniform was comforting as Hannah followed Vanhiller up the stairs. She hoped she'd see Betsy, despite what Vanhiller had said earlier about her moving east. She soon discovered that her "room" was actually a cramped dormitory with six cots, five of them already occupied. The room was sparsely furnished otherwise. A full-length mirror leaned against the far wall, and next to it was an armoire with hatboxes stacked on top.

Vanhiller twirled his cane between his fingers, nodding his head as if satisfied. The gaslight sconce was turned low, but not so low that Hannah couldn't see that an older woman had tearstains on her cheeks. She counted five females ranging in age from about fifteen to fifty or more, all dressed in similar cotton nightgowns. They looked up indifferently as she entered. Betsy was not among them. Hesitant to show the least anxiety, she turned toward Vanhiller and mimicked her warmest smile. "Thank you so much. I can't wait to get started tomorrow."

Her heartbeat quickened and she swallowed hard. Everything about the expressions of the others, except possibly the youngest one, told her that the Venus flytrap had snapped shut on its latest victim. Who had previously occupied this cot? And where was she now?

Hannah remembered the bars on the windows, hidden from inside view by the drawn shades. Had these women given up, or would she find an ally among them? What "training" did Vanhiller offer? She had the feeling that whatever it was, she was not going to like it.

She sat on the edge of the cot and looked around. "I'm Hannah," she half whispered. A couple of the women mumbled their names inaudibly, and the others didn't bother to answer. "Maybe tomorrow," she said, more to herself than anyone else. Were they disinterested, or did Vanhiller keep such a tight rein on them that they spoke only when he wanted them to?

Vanhiller lowered the gaslight flame to a bare flicker that did little to illuminate the room. He shut the door.

Hannah was sure that she heard the metallic clack of a bolt

sliding into place. Now there were two locked doors between her and freedom. She slid her basket under the cot and lay down facing the tearstained woman. She reached out and placed her hand over the woman's. It felt stiff and disfigured with arthritis. "Are you all right?"

"You can't stay here," she whispered. "The first chance you get, run."

Hannah had guessed as much already. "What's your name?"

"Lily."

"It's going to be all right, Lily. We'll go together. I'll help you."

Lily's eyes glistened with tears. "It's too late for me. But you may have a chance."

There was a thud on the wall from the other side. "What's that?" Hannah whispered.

"It's Lucas. He sleeps in a chair in the hall. He keeps us safe."

Hannah scoffed. "Are you sure he isn't keeping us from leaving, Lily?" She hesitated. "Lily? Was Betsy Day here?"

"You two shut up. I need to sleep." Although Hannah hadn't heard her voice before, she realized that the admonishment came from the direction of the youngest one.

Ignoring her, Hannah asked, "Who is that? What's her story?"

Lily put her finger to her lips and shook her head. "Be careful around Iris. She's dangerous." She shut her eyes in an obvious dismissal of the conversation.

Hannah listened until the room grew silent save for the sounds of breathing and soft snores. She could see that Lily's shoulders moved in rhythm to soft sobs. "Lily, was Betsy Day here?"

Lily's eyes grew wide, and her mouth grimaced. "Don't ever mention her again. Do you understand? Not ever. You must forget her."

Hannah rolled onto her back, staring into the abyss. She had a sinking feeling in the pit of her stomach. Betsy hadn't gone to

New York City as Vanhiller said. Betsy hadn't come for her because she couldn't. Hannah knew that now. Betsy was dead, probably by his hand or that of his poor brother, Lucas.

Hannah thought Lily must be too terrified to confide in her. Then she wondered if Lily might try to curry favor with Vanhiller by informing on Hannah. *Probably not*, Hannah thought, but she didn't know yet about the others. Lily had warned her about Iris, but were there others she should be concerned about?

Hannah promised herself that she would find out about Betsy, whatever the risks.

4

Cabot Falls, Vermont
Present Day

Sofia determined to make the best of the Founder's Day project, even if it meant dealing with Norton. The next day, Sofia saw that he had covered his store window with heavy paper. It wasn't unusual to do that in preparing for grand openings, but it seemed ominous as she recalled those two rough-looking men from yesterday. Norton's expression hadn't been angry. He had looked worried, even frightened.

Vanessa and Wynter were helping the Pinot Painters get their booth ready. Jim had a meeting at the fire station, and Luke, Matthew, and Bryce decided to watch booth construction and play some catch on the green. Sofia was eager to paint the sandwich-style sign Jim had made. She could put it on the sidewalk when the shop was open and bring it in when she was closed.

The Andersons had ordered a red-and-white-striped awning, which was scheduled for installation today. With the bistro tables and chairs, it would provide the perfect ambiance of an Italian sidewalk café.

The installers arrived soon after she opened the shop and took the better part of the morning to finish. Sofia finished the sign, then ran hot water into a bucket with disinfecting soap and scrubbed the preparation counters, humming as she worked.

Suddenly, the volume of construction noise coming from the square cut through her concentration. Sofia put down her scrub brush and rushed to the door to see what was going on. "Oh no!"

Flames shot into the air and black smoke billowed. Several of the booths were on fire, and grown-ups and children of all ages were running in every direction, shouting. Moments later, the howl and clang of the fire trucks broke through the noise. Sofia felt as if her heart would stop. "The kids!" She had pulled the shop door closed and had started toward the square when she saw them coming toward her.

Sofia let her breath out in relief, but the relief was short-lived. "Matthew! Where's Matthew?"

Luke jerked his head around. "He was right behind us. Matthew?"

The fire trucks stopped with a whooshing of hydraulic brakes. The firemen scrambled down and moved to attach the hose to the hydrant.

"Go to the shop and stay there!" Sofia shouted to her children. "Matthew! Matthew! Where are you?" She broke into a run, pushing through the crowd that was moving in the opposite direction.

"He's here, Mrs. Parker," called a voice in the melee. It was Ryan Quimby, a Cabot Falls policeman who was familiar to Sofia.

"Oh, thank you!" Sofia said. She wrapped her arms around Matthew. "Thank God! I was so scared."

The flames had vanished and the smoke had all but disappeared. The crowds soon returned to watch the aftermath as the volunteers rolled up their hoses and sifted through the hot residue.

"Come with me, Matthew," Sofia said, taking his hand.

"I'm afraid not, Mrs. Parker," Officer Quimby said, reaching a hand out and taking Matthew's shoulder.

"What?" Sofia saw the officer's grim expression. "What do you mean?"

Matthew burst into tears.

"I'm s-sorry, Mrs. Parker," the young officer said.

Sofia was aware that he stuttered only when he was nervous. She braced herself for bad news.

"Matthew has to come to the station with me. I'm afraid he's responsible for the fire."

Matthew broke away from the officer's grip and wrapped his arms around Sofia, burying his face against her. "I . . . I didn't, Mom!"

"Officer Quimby," Sofia said, recovering from her momentary shock, "you must be mistaken. Let's go back to the shop, and we'll get to the bottom of this quickly."

The rest of the brood was inside the shop, huddled in quiet conversation. They looked up, wide-eyed and openmouthed, as the trio walked in. "Now, Officer Quimby, tell me why you are accusing Matthew of causing the fire. Surely you don't think he's the town arsonist! That's ludicrous."

"No ma'am, just this fire. I was directing traffic a few blocks away when I heard what sounded like firecrackers and bottle rockets. By the time I got there, the booths were on fire, and I saw Matthew holding matches and more bottle rockets. I can't say until the official investigation, of course, but the evidence looks bad. If it shows the fire started from bottle rockets—"

"I get the gist of it," Sofia said. "But please, wait until they determine the cause, and I promise, if that's the case, I'll personally bring him to the station."

"I can do that, Mrs. Parker," Officer Quimby said. He reached over and patted Matthew on the shoulder. "Sorry, Matthew. I know you're a good kid. I'm sure it was an accident, but there are no fireworks allowed, except by the professionals." And with that, he left.

Sofia felt hot tears fall on her cheeks. She had such mixed emotions: anger, fear, confusion. She turned to the kids. "Matthew is old enough to know better, but you boys were supposed to keep an eye on him. What was so important that you couldn't do one simple thing, like watching him?"

Bryce looked pale. Sofia could only imagine that he was worried that his name would somehow get connected to this and it might hurt his father's campaign. But she couldn't think about that now. She realized that Matthew was impulsive, but this was beyond anything he'd ever done.

Jim, still in his firefighter gear, stuck his head in. "Everything all right? I saw Officer Quimby leave here."

"I'll explain later. Will you take the kids home and—"

The Parker children interrupted with protests, but she held up her hand. "Not another word from any of you. We'll talk when I get home. I need to finish up here."

When she finished cleaning, she stowed the bucket and brush in the closet and walked outside, ready to head home. She saw that a small crowd had gathered in front of Norton's shop, snickering at the crudely painted sign in his window: "A New U. Lose the Fat U Gain Next Door." Norton stood in the doorway, smirking. "It's free speech!" he told Sofia.

"Nothing in life is free, Mr. Norton!" Sofia snapped. "The sooner you learn that, the better off you'll be."

"You heard her, folks! She threatened me!" Norton yelled.

Sofia walked to her Suburban and climbed in. This project had turned into a nightmare, and she had an even worse one waiting for her at home.

Chicago, Illinois
Summer 1867

What more could possibly go wrong? Hannah wondered as she cradled the pink quilt in her arms. She fell asleep listening to the sounds of breathing, a sound so familiar after years of life at the orphanage. She sat up at the sound of the bolt sliding back. The door opened and Vanhiller, already looking dapper in a tailor-fitted brown suit, struck the floor with the heel of his cane.

"Up and ready, ladies. Donors are waiting. Hurry, hurry, hurry!"

The others scrambled from their cots and hastily smoothed the sheets. Hannah followed their lead. "The water closet is two doors away," Lily offered. She flung open the armoire, revealing an array of the finest day dresses Hannah had ever seen. She stared in awe. Hatboxes were stacked on top of one another on the shelves, and colorful parasols and drawstring purses hung on hooks attached inside both doors.

"I'm Hannah," she said to the one she knew to be Iris.

"Uh-huh." Iris didn't even glance at her as she wiggled into a dress that looked too old for her. She grabbed a pair of nice shoes and sat on her cot to buckle them. She seemed to relish playing dress-up.

Lily had returned. She wore a demure, dark blue gabardine dress with a bustle. She had already twisted her graying hair into a bun at the back of her neck.

"Do I just pick a dress?" Hannah asked. They all appeared to be stylish and not gray checked, which was a plus.

"Oh no," Lily said, shaking her head vigorously. She picked a black parasol off the door hook and turned toward Iris. "You have my purse."

"You won't need it," Iris said with a smirk.

Lily gasped and her face went pale. "What have you heard?" Iris shrugged, snickering, and exited the room.

"Lily, do I choose any dress?" Hannah repeated, anxious to snap Lily out of what looked like an anxiety attack in the making.

"No . . . uh, no," Lily said. "Carlton will let you know. Come downstairs now. We need to eat. Stay close. And don't speak."

Hannah wasn't sure if staying close was for her protection or Lily's. She followed Lily down the stairs, making mental notes of which stairs squeaked.

The kitchen smelled of eggs and sausage. Millie was busily filling plates as the women carried them to the table. When they were all seated, Vanhiller said, "Ladies, Hannah is joining us. Introduce yourselves, and welcome her."

The first to speak up was Autumn; Hannah recognized her now. She had been twelve years old when Autumn aged out of the orphanage. That would make her only twenty-four, yet she had frown wrinkles on her forehead and a V-shaped wrinkle between her eyebrows. Her mouth sagged at the corners like a reverse smile. *Could six years have aged her that much?* Hannah wondered.

Autumn flinched visibly when Vanhiller called her name. "Carlton takes care of us." Her voice was stilted and without inflection. "I had no skills when I left the orphanage, but he taught me everything I know."

Vanhiller nodded, obviously pleased that she had performed as he wished. "Victoria here was widowed young, and I saw her begging on the street, turned out of her home. Tell her, Victoria."

"It is true," Victoria said. "I was arrested many times for loitering until Carlton took me in." She glanced sideways at him. "I am so grateful that I have a home here." Her lower lip quivered slightly.

Hannah felt sure that Victoria was lying and afraid. "And what do you do?" she asked as casually as she could manage.

Victoria's mouth flew open, and she flashed an anxious look at Vanhiller as he cleared his throat and said, "Cadence? Your turn."

Cadence looked only a little older than Hannah. She stared at her plate as she mumbled, "My husband didn't return after the war."

"Ladies, it's time to go to work," Vanhiller said. "Save the rest of the introductions until this evening. Lucas and Millie will watch over you today. I'll stay here and get Hannah started." The women rose almost in unison. "Not you, Lily," he said. "Your production has been low lately. It's time for a refresher course. Or retirement."

Lily paled. "I'll do better, Carlton, I promise!"

"We'll see," Vanhiller said. He reached out to touch her shoulder as she shrank back. "Go to the workroom, ladies." He swept the air with his hand, showing the way, just as Millie bustled into the kitchen and gathered up the plates. "Leave them for now, dear," he instructed. "You are needed at the station today."

She nodded, releasing the bow that kept her apron in place. She quickly placed it on the wall hook and hurried away.

Hannah wondered what station Vanhiller referred to. He had told the others that Millie and Lucas would accompany them this morning; he hadn't said where. She patted Lily's hand as they walked down the hall and turned into the room full of mannequins. Lily's face was damp with tears, a sign of severe stress. Could it be fear of Vanhiller?

Vanhiller sat on the wooden park bench. "All right, Lily. Show me that you still have the skills I taught you."

"I-I need a moment, Carlton," Lily told him. "I'm so nervous."

"Now now, Lily, all I'm asking is for you to do your best." He motioned for Hannah to sit on the bench beside him. "Watch and learn—perhaps."

Hannah took a seat and watched with curiosity. If she was not altering the garments, what were the mannequins for?

Lily rubbed her hands together fitfully. She picked up a parasol leaning against the wall and walked toward one of the figures. Stumbling into it slightly, she muttered apologetically as she reached into its coat pocket. A bell rang.

Vanhiller jumped up, moaning, "Lily, Lily, Lily, what did I tell you?"

Hannah sat dumbfounded, reviewing what she had just witnessed in disbelief. Could it be true that Vanhiller had plucked these women, each down on her luck for a different reason, and with promises of a better life, trained them in sleight of hand? Carlton Vanhiller, with the help of his intimidated wife and his unwitting brother, was running a ring of pickpockets?

Hannah wanted no part of this. She had to get away. But how could she do so without arousing suspicion? Remembering those intriguing news articles about the Pinkerton agency, she asked herself, *What would the Chameleon do?*

Whatever she did next would set in motion consequences on which her very life depended. She closed her eyes and prayed for wisdom.

5

Cabot Falls, Vermont
Present Day

atthew and Jessop Norton are two different issues, Sofia reminded herself. *I can't let my feelings about either one cloud the other.* She stepped inside her home.

Jim looked up from slicing onions. The sight of him wearing scuba goggles broke through her thoughts, and she managed a laugh. "Where's Matthew?"

"In his room with the door shut. He hasn't said a word. Is Officer Quimby positive that Matthew caused the fire?" He set down the knife and held out his arms to her.

Sofia stepped into his embrace. "He's scared. I just want to hold him tightly and tell him that it'll be all right. That we'll get through this."

"Your instincts are right on, Sofia. Poor little guy may be too scared to talk to us right now."

Sofia nodded, breaking the embrace. "I need to bake something, or I'll go ballistic." She told him about Norton's mocking sign and his accusation that she had threatened him.

She baked red velvet cupcakes while Jim prepared cookout food. Except for Matthew, who had refused to join them, the Parkers and Bryce ate by the tent and toasted marshmallows for s'mores.

The boys offered little help in unraveling the earlier events, as they had been at the far end of the square. Fergus, their border collie, settled into the tent with them.

Sofia took a plate to Matthew. Although he turned his face toward his pillow, she sat on the edge of the bed and placed her hand on his shoulder. "When you're ready to talk, I'm ready to listen, Matthew. But you must eventually talk. We're a family, and we stick together. We will work through it, okay?"

Before retiring for the night, Sofia checked the computer to see if anyone had answered her query about the initials on the pink quilt square. Neither her sisters nor aunts had any clues. A research librarian at the Smithsonian wrote that a Hannah Reed was on the roster of the Pinkerton Detective Agency from late 1867 through 1871. Sofia still didn't know what she had to do with the quilt square or the initials A.J. But since the diary she had inherited with the quilt listed her, it must be important to consider, at least until she could eliminate her or discover her connection.

Jim was already asleep when Sofia slipped into bed, her head filled with questions about the past and present. It seemed that she had no sooner fallen asleep than the bedside phone and Jim's cell phone rang simultaneously.

"Fire call," Jim said as Sofia sat bolt upright in bed. "Sofia, the address is the block the shops are on."

Sofia dressed and gathered her wits before she woke Vanessa and told her the situation. "You're in charge."

As she headed out the door, she looked toward the square. The night sky glowed bright red. Losing those shops would be devastating.

Sofia abandoned the Suburban two blocks from the square

and broke into a run toward the shops. The volunteers had confined the fire to the two shops on the end: Norton's and La Dolce Vita. Norton had already arrived. He paced up and down, wailing miserably.

Suddenly, the A New U window exploded, sending shattered glass into the street. Someone screamed, "Look! Someone's in there!" The flames illuminated a figure in the middle of stationary bikes, treadmills, and stair-climber machines.

The fire chief leaped through the opening and brought out what turned out to be a mannequin. "Why didn't you tell me you had a store dummy in your shop?" he demanded of Norton. "I could've been killed going in there."

"I wasn't thinking. Just look at my shop! It was probably that Parker woman."

While the volunteers extinguished the fire, Sofia could do nothing but sit on the curb and watch. It was nearly dawn before it was cool enough to step inside the charred businesses. The wall between La Dolce Vita and A New U was severely burned. While the remainder of the structure was stable and the outer wall was sound, the insides of both shops were covered in soot.

Mayor Goodson stood inside the yellow tape with his cell phone to his ear. He motioned for the local TV crew. "Construction workers from surrounding towns will be here by ten this morning. We will not cancel the celebration. If I know the people of Cabot Falls, they will all pitch in."

Sofia's shoulders sagged. "I don't know, Jim. The mayor sounds positive. But I just don't know if I can do this."

"It looks worse than it is. Some soap and water and a few sheets of drywall will work wonders. I can't say the same about Norton's business. All those machines look twisted, and I'm sure the motors are finished. It's just his luck to have brought everything in before this. What a loss."

"Uh-huh." Sofia nodded absently. She was staring at something on the kitchen counter. "Jim, why would the volunteers pull out the bucket and brush?"

"They wouldn't. Why?"

"Because I put everything back in the closet before I left this afternoon." She lifted the bucket. There was no soot under it. "Jim, someone was in here. This fire was deliberate."

Her phone rang. It was Vanessa. "Mom, I've looked everywhere. Matthew is missing."

Chicago, Illinois
Summer 1867

Hannah felt the blood drain from her face. It was as if her throat were closing on her. It was difficult to breathe. Vanhiller had lured her to his home with promises of helping her adjust to life outside the orphanage. Instead, he obviously intended to train her as part of his band of female pickpockets that he had named Six of Hearts.

Jaw slack with shock, she watched as he scolded Lily for setting off a bell in the mannequin's pocket. "That is exceedingly sloppy, Lily."

Lily cringed. "I . . . I'll do better. My hands hurt so bad, Carlton. Perhaps if I took a powder I could do this. There would be a lot of distractions in big crowds, so I'm sure the mark wouldn't notice."

Vanhiller narrowed his eyes and sighed deeply. "If the bell sounds, it is a sign that a real mark would feel it. You are of no use to me anymore."

Hannah leaped up, hoping to distract Vanhiller from Lily, at least for now. "Carlton, please show me the proper technique. Perhaps Lily could tend to her hands while you show me." She wondered how long Lily had been here. This was a horrible life, but what life would she have if he turned her out? She shuddered. Perhaps that wasn't the worst fate his gang of thieves faced when they were no longer useful. She could only hope that the cot she now occupied had belonged to an escapee.

He let go of Lily's arm and turned toward Hannah, grinning. "Ah, an eager student. Yes, of course."

Lily skittered off toward the kitchen as Vanhiller motioned for Hannah to join him by the mannequin. "Each of these marks—"

"Marks?" Hannah asked.

He scowled, obviously annoyed at the interruption. "Save your questions, Hannah. Didn't they teach you at the orphanage not to interrupt? Yes, mark—that is what we call the donor. He is *marked* for a contribution, see?"

Hannah swallowed her astonishment. *Donor? Contribution? The word is victim*, she thought. She nodded with her best smile as he continued.

"It takes practice to have a light touch. Practice you will get in this room. You will use any means to distract the mark while you lift his wallet or watch or a woman's cash or jewelry." He smiled and cupped her chin in his hand. "Pretty, flawless face, huge blue eyes with a look of pure innocence, even a sprinkle of freckles on the bridge of your nose . . . yes, you'll do nicely. What man wouldn't be distracted? Of course, you mustn't forget the female marks. You women make such a fuss about wanting equal rights."

Hannah shoved her fists into the skirt pockets so he wouldn't notice her white knuckles. She wondered if Vanhiller ever put himself in harm's way or if he considered himself superior and irreplaceable. How many women were spending time in prison after being caught doing his dirty work? "Don't the, uh, donors, miss their belongings and report it?" she asked. "They might remember being jostled and point us out to the authorities." Perhaps she should advise Lily to allow herself to be caught. Surely prison would be no worse than this unholy place.

"We work the train stations and near the transportation depots. By the time they realize their loss, they are far away with no idea when or where they lost it. Even if they recall, it is too late to catch up with us."

Hannah hid her dismay and empathy for the poor victims. She knew what it was like to be in a strange place with no means. "Yes, I see how one might become skilled in picking pockets or even slipping a piece of jewelry away. But a lady's handbag can hold only so much. We couldn't possibly hide more than a couple of items." She felt like a detective prying facts from a culprit. But the more she knew, the more likely she could get away.

Vanhiller snorted. "Do you know the capacity of a closed parasol? Iris once brought home ten men's wallets, four gold watches with chains intact, and a lady's pearl necklace, and all of them secured in her parasol without a telltale bulge or gaping spines." He hooked his thumbs beneath his lapels. "That young girl is my star pupil. And she enjoys her work. She'll be around a long time."

Hannah followed his cue and smiled, nodding in agreement. He was prideful—one of the seven deadly sins, she recalled from Sunday school. He considered it a strength. She would make it his weakness. That could be his downfall. It would take time, though. She wondered how much time Lily had. She decided to play into his fantasy about himself.

"A prestidigitator," she cooed, although it nauseated her to praise him. "The summa cum laude of the school of pocket-picking, king of the sleight of hand, master of legerdemain . . . what a grand teacher you must be." That was as many praiseworthy descriptions for his thievery as her reading had afforded her. It would have to do. Other words that came to mind were *perpetrator, crook, criminal,* and *potential prisoner.* But her flattery seemed to do the trick as he puffed up like a rooster about to welcome daylight.

"You will do well, Hannah." He pulled his pocket watch and tapped its face, then twisted the tiny knob. "Now, let's go find you some proper clothing for your lessons."

She didn't have to feign joy at that suggestion. Hannah followed Vanhiller up the stairs. She thought that as long as she could hold his attention, he wouldn't be threatening Lily. The poor woman was nearly beside herself, and who could blame her?

As she traipsed up the steps, she wondered how long she'd have to keep up her charade before she could make her escape. She deliberately stepped hard on the creaky steps. There was no need to worry about giving herself away.

Vanhiller flung open the armoire and pulled out a gray morning dress, then shoved it back onto the hanger. "No, you have had enough gray, have you not? How about this one? It is nice lavender, the color of wisteria. With that auburn hair, you'd be impressive."

Caught up in the moment, Hannah sucked in her breath at the sight of the taffeta dress. It was the most beautiful dress she'd ever seen. "Oh, what about this one?" Not that she had for one moment forgotten her situation, but the array of clothes was irresistible and as far from gray check as she could get.

"No, that is more suitable for evening wear. Perhaps when you do well with your training, you can attend a gala event and wear this. You can collect quite a bit as you whirl around the dance floor." He pulled a deep purple gabardine dress from the armoire. "This one does not have the bright colors you are drawn to, but for now, it will do. You may accessorize it as you see fit, and then join me downstairs in the workroom."

Hannah shut the door and changed into the plum dress. She stood in front of the full-length mirror and stared at the strange image. The skirt fell in folds that stopped just short of the floor, and the bodice clung to her slender figure with a false peplum so it resembled a suit. Was that the real Hannah looking back at her?

The uniforms at Whiteside made the message clear: None of the girls was the least bit special. They dressed alike, walked in lines, and had no unique features. But this—*oh my!* She balanced on her tiptoes and rummaged through the hatboxes until she found a hat the same color. She giggled. It looked as if a little bird had just landed on a flapjack covered in grape syrup. She twisted her braids into a bun and pinned them. Then she placed the hat on her head tilted to one side and forward, pushing the long hatpin through to hold it in place.

When she had selected a dark, taffeta-covered parasol, she twirled in front of the mirror. She ran her hand down the flared skirt; her fingers caught on an opening. Examining the skirt more closely, Hannah discovered pockets hidden in the folds. The outfit had been modified to stash away the stolen items quickly.

Vanhiller had thought of everything. She selected a handbag of crushed velvet and joined her new "employer" in the workroom. She smiled at him, feigning eagerness to learn from the master. Yet her thoughts were about that locked door and how she could escape safely.

He nodded his obvious approval. "Perfect," he said.

Hannah forced a giggle and twirled as if basking in his approval. "I doubt anyone would suspect such an elegant lady as a thief." She giggled again, hoping to convince him that she was eager to please him.

Obviously happy, he said, "Don't think of yourself as a thief. You are merely relieving the donors of the dilemma of how to spend their money. We are doing them a favor. Our skills are those of a magician, an illusionist. You call his attention to here"—Vanhiller lifted his cane and waggled it—"while you ply your trade here." He triumphantly waved the pocket watch he had removed from the mannequin without the hint of a bell.

"Oh, that was marvelous!" Hannah cooed. "It is simply masterful!" She grinned, imagining him as a peacock in full plumage as he casually rolled his cane through his fingers.

"I will teach you, Hannah." He took her hand in his and stroked it tenderly. "You have long, nimble fingers and small, delicate hands. In other circumstances, you might have been a pianist or a harpist. But they are perfect for surreptitiously unburdening our donors." His mustache wiggled like a woolly caterpillar as he broke into a grin.

Hannah threw back her head in a mocking laugh designed to convince Vanhiller that she was a willing student. She would practice sleight of hand until she was perfect.

Vanhiller, without being any the wiser, was going to help her escape. She would simply lift the key from Millie's skirt pocket. Even the Chameleon would be impressed with her plan.

The hardest part of the plan was not to get caught.

6

*H*ot tears streamed down Sofia's cheeks. "Matthew is missing!" she yelled to Jim and ran to her SUV, leaving him to follow in his own car.

By the time she reached home, Bryce and Luke were scouring the nearby woods, and Vanessa and Wynter were searching the basement, closets, under beds, and inside kitchen cabinets—any place large enough to conceal a ten-year-old boy.

Pat and Homer Cooper, still wearing their house slippers and robes, joined them with flashlights, calling out to Matthew.

"I should have realized how traumatized he was," Sofia moaned. "I should—"

"Now, don't you worry," Pat said. "We'll find him. I don't believe Matthew would go far. Maybe you should call the police, though, so they can issue a Code Adam."

"Code Adam!" Sofia gasped.

"Now Pat, you're upsetting Sofia with your cop talk," Homer said. "Matthew has not been abducted. He's just hiding, that's all."

"Code Adam isn't just for abduction, Homer. It's for missing children."

Sofia left the Coopers to sort out their differences and headed toward Norton's property. The garage was open, and she aimed her flashlight into the shadows. There was the chassis of a vintage sports car, but nothing else except several cases of charcoal starter fluid, a grill, and two bags of charcoal briquettes. She circled his house and the next yard. The Gregory family was on vacation, so she didn't bother to knock.

She returned to her yard to find Luke with Fergus. "Find Matthew," he said. "Go now, find Matthew."

Fergus barked and chased his tail before racing around the yard, yipping in his high-pitched tone. He circled the tree and tent, leaping and snapping at the air.

"Put that ridiculous dog in the house," Sofia told Luke. "He's only in the way and a distraction."

Jim drove up. "Nothing yet? Matthew was really upset, especially with another fire in town. He's probably just hiding nearby. But the fire volunteers are coming. They'll start on the other side of the woods and come this way. The police are tied up with the fire investigation. If we don't find him in a little while, I'm calling the state police with the dogs."

Sofia's tears burst forth like floodwaters through a levee. "Oh, Jim, I . . . I . . ."

"Honey, why don't you make a pot of coffee and put out some of those muffins you've been baking?" Jim said. He squeezed her hand reassuringly. "It will be okay. Matthew wouldn't deliberately do anything to hurt us. He's just confused, and he doesn't know how to deal with it."

Sofia nodded, grateful to feel useful. She pushed Fergus back as she entered the kitchen. "Oh no you don't!" she told the dog. "You stay in here, out of the way." She pulled out the tall urn and set the coffee to perking. "Muffins . . . muffins," she mumbled. She opened the freezer to retrieve a box of lemon poppyseed muffins, but they were missing. Missing boy; missing muffins. For some reason, the combination offered her a bit of comfort.

Fergus whimpered and scratched at the door. "Not now," Sofia said. "Settle down." Fergus barked and resumed whimpering.

"What, you silly dog?" Sofia scolded as she pulled paper cups from the cabinet. "You would just be in the way out there."

The coffee ceased perking, and Sofia unplugged it. She opened the screen door to carry it out to the picnic table, and Fergus rushed through the door ahead of her, racing to the large oak tree, where he circled and sat at the foot of the tree, barking. It was the one in which the boys had been building their tree house. They had constructed only a floor before Norton got an injunction to stop it. The rope ladder was missing.

Sofia retrieved the extension ladder from Jim's workshop and leaned it against the tree. When she reached the top, there was Matthew, sleeping atop his bedroll, surrounded by muffin wrappers. She shook him gently. "Come on, honey. It's time to come home."

When she had Matthew safely on the ground, she rang the dinner bell to call the searchers back. She served coffee and slices of gingerbread with maple syrup and thanked them for their help.

"You're forgetting someone, Mom," Luke said. "You yelled at Fergus, but he was trying to tell us where Matthew was the whole time."

Sofia laughed. "You're right, Luke. Fergus, I apologize for not understanding dog-speak. You get an extra sweet-potato chip in your bowl, okay?"

Fergus wagged all over and leaped up, snapping at the air.

Sofia decided to tackle the six-hundred pound gorilla in the room. "Okay, Matthew, we need to talk. We're all here to help. Neighbors, even guys who didn't know you, were looking for you. That's a sign that we're not your enemy, right? So you're going to talk with us—no more silent treatment. And then we will all figure out how to get the shop back in order for the celebration. Is everyone agreed?"

She didn't wait for an answer. "Okay, let's do this!" She felt as if she had her family on the right track once more. As for herself, she wasn't sure. After all, Norton had shouted for everyone to hear that she had threatened him. And now his shop was in ruins. Even with Matthew back, she had never felt so frightened.

Chicago, Illinois
Summer 1867

Hannah had never felt so frightened. She had no choice but to practice under Vanhiller's watchful eyes. His words were warm and encouraging, in contrast to his cold, dark eyes. She had never stared into the mouth of a cave, straining to see the danger that might wait beyond the darkness. But she imagined that it must be like looking into his eyes, fearing that what she couldn't see lurking there was ready to strike, like the snake that had inspired the cane he carried.

She turned toward the door at the sound of shuffling feet on the wood floors. The women, herded by Millie and Lucas, were home. Millie removed her hat as she bustled past them and moved toward the kitchen. Lucas, hat in hand, lingered in the workroom doorway with a look of anticipation until Vanhiller acknowledged him with a nod.

Iris elbowed her way through the others and triumphantly waved an ebony cameo framed in gold with a glitter of surrounding diamonds. "That woman asked for it," she said. Her face contorted into a triumphant grin. "Her and her haughty ways. I just wish I could have relieved her of her earrings too."

Carter spread a dark cloth on the park bench, and Iris pulled pocketbooks, coin purses, and jewelry from her skirt pockets. She held her parasol upside down over the cloth, and several pocket watches tumbled onto the pile.

"Very good, Iris," Vanhiller said. "I can always depend on you."

Grinning triumphantly, Iris sashayed to the rear of the group as each woman presented her day's work. Autumn hung back. Her face was flushed as Vanhiller wiggled his finger, signaling her to approach.

"I-I'm sorry, Carlton," she stammered as she added only a few pieces to the pile. "I-I was being watched. I tried, but Iris pushed in ahead of me. I'm sorry. I'll do bet—"

Carter shook his head and tsk-tsked. "Of course you will do better, Autumn. But you know what happens next."

Autumn hung her head. "Yes sir."

Hannah could feel her heart pounding against her rib cage. What were they talking about? Did he intend to punish her for bad luck? How? She had seen the terror in Lily's eyes as she contemplated her future. Autumn was trembling.

"Lucas!" Vanhiller shouted, and the clumsy older brother appeared almost immediately at the door. "Autumn missed her quota today. She needs to think about it undisturbed."

Autumn broke into tears, pleading as Lucas guided her from the room.

"Where are you taking her?" Hannah demanded.

"Not to worry, Hannah." Vanhiller rubbed the smooth top of the snake head as he spoke. "She will merely spend time in the thinking room. No harm comes to my ladies."

It wasn't until he led them to the kitchen for their supper of potato soup that she fully understood what he meant by "the thinking room." As he steered the crew of pickpockets down the hall, Hannah heard soft sobs from what she had thought was secured storage under the stairs. *It must be dark and hot and cramped beyond belief in there. What kind of a person does that to another?* Vanhiller was a monster, and she gritted her teeth to keep from saying anything. It was even more imperative than she had first thought to get out of there and to help the others escape too. There were more of them than of their captors. Could they not overwhelm them?

She had never seen Vanhiller without his deadly carved cane, and she doubted that he would hesitate to use it if he felt threatened. Lucas seemed clumsy, but he was large, perhaps powerful. Did he carry a weapon beneath that ill-fitting coat?

She stared at Autumn's empty chair at the table. Did Vanhiller intend to starve and terrify her into bringing him more wealth? She looked at the other faces. They offered no clue as to their thoughts. Were they so subdued after months—even years—in his service that they were devoid of empathy for Autumn? Perhaps they had all experienced the "thinking room" so that they feared it more than they had compassion for another human.

Lily kept her eyes focused on her bowl. If Vanhiller was angry with Autumn for so little success today, what did he feel about Lily, who had produced nothing? Iris, who had won Vanhiller's praise for the bounty she brought, received the most generous portion of soup, Hannah noticed. Vanhiller doled out reward and punishment according to the loot they produced.

Patience, she told herself. Vanhiller would receive his comeuppance if she had anything to say about it.

After supper, Lucas herded the women like cattle up the steps and to the dormitory to be shut in for the night. Autumn's bed remained empty. Hannah hugged her silk quilt to her, although its soft folds offered little comfort. She fell asleep staring beyond it to Lily's sleeping form. Sometime during the night, she stirred, vaguely aware of movement nearby. The quilt slipped from her arms and slid to the floor, settling with a soft whooshing sound. Exhausted, she eased back into sleep and didn't wake until daylight.

Hannah blinked blearily as light penetrated her eyelids. Gradually focusing, she realized what she was seeing—or, more accurately, what she was not seeing. She bolted from the cot and looked around the room as the others stretched and straightened their sheets. "Where's Lily?"

The others seemed to freeze in place except for their heads swiveling in search of the older woman. The door was still closed.

Hannah pounded on the door. "Open the door! Where's Lily?"

"Stop it!" Iris yelled. "You're going to get all of us in trouble. Shut up about Lily."

Hannah stepped back as she heard the bolt slide on the other side of the door. She pushed past Lucas, calling out to Lily. There was no answer. She whirled and stalked back to Lucas, grabbing his jacket by the lapels. "Where is she? Where is Lily?"

Lucas blinked at her as if he didn't comprehend and then shook his head slowly. "Carlton don't like it when you yell, Hannah. He don't like it. You gotta stop."

She balled her fists angrily. "I won't stop until you tell me what you did to her."

Lucas grabbed both of Hannah's wrists. "You gotta stop, Hannah. Please."

Hannah drew back, stunned by his plea. His expression was one of concern that bordered on genuine fear. Was he afraid for her or for himself? She thought she knew the answer. *Lily has outlived her usefulness, and she's been discarded like trash.* Had Vanhiller done the same to her friend Betsy?

Had Lucas murdered her on Vanhiller's orders? Or did he merely get rid of the evidence for his brother? What kind of hold did Vanhiller have on his brother? Hannah nodded her understanding to Lucas, and he let her go.

She washed up and soon joined the others at the table. Autumn was there. They ate in silence. Hannah was aware that Vanhiller was watching them carefully. She believed he was especially focused on her. She dared to return his gaze.

When the others left for their day's "collections," as Vanhiller called them, he put Hannah to work on making her own collection. When she had successfully managed to retrieve four wallets and a pocket watch without setting off the bells, she pretended to be pleased. "Am I ready to join the others?" she asked. It was the only way she would ever get outside the locked door.

He rubbed the snake head and smiled. "Oh, my eager little student, not so fast. It is one thing to succeed with the mannequins. But it is quite another to stealthily collect from a live donor—me!"

Hannah pretended excitement and embraced him, then jumped back apologetically. "Oh, I'm so sorry. I was excited. I didn't mean to offend you."

"Quite all right, my dear Hannah. I am pleased that you are such a quick learner and so eager to prove your mettle. Now, for the test—"

"Oh, but you see, I have already passed it," Hannah said. She dangled his diamond stickpin and his pocket watch in front of him.

Vanhiller's mouth flew open in an expression of shock, and with his free hand, he patted his tie and watch pocket. He seemed torn between embarrassment at having his student outsmart him and pride in having taught her well. "I do believe that you have surpassed Iris," he said. "That is quite a feat. I can't wait to see you in action."

"At the train station?" Hannah asked. Her thoughts turned to ways she might escape. She had never been to any of the stations, but she imagined huge crowds of milling passengers coming and going, perhaps a policeman or two to keep order or watch for criminals. Perhaps she could mingle and disappear into the crowd, breaking away in a dead run. Could she find a policeman quickly? Would he believe her as she blurted out her story?

But the scenarios she created in her mind always ended up with Vanhiller or his brother catching her, perhaps telling the police that she was a runaway, a lunatic. She shuddered, imagining herself shoved into the dark hole under the stairs, unable to stand or stretch, denied food. She needed a better plan.

Vanhiller took back his stickpin and inserted it into his dark blue silk tie. He replaced his pocket watch, hooking the chain securely through the small slit and patting it. "Not the train station, my dear. I have something much better in mind for you."

Hannah felt a chill slither up her spine and prickle her neck. What could he be thinking? She imagined her lifeless body lying next to Lily's and Betsy's. There would be no one to mourn her.

7

Cabot Falls, Vermont
Present Day

What can I say that might help? Sofia wondered as she tucked Matthew in. The day had been long, and everyone was bone-weary by the time they finally got into bed. When Sophia leaned over to kiss him good night, he wrapped his arms around her neck. "Mom, I'm sorry!"

"I know, Matthew. You scared all of us. Why the tree, of all places?"

"You said we can't leave the yard after dark; I didn't want to make you any madder than you were already." Matthew scooted over to make room for her to sit beside him.

"I wasn't mad. I was disappointed that you wouldn't talk about it. Where did you get the fireworks, anyway?"

"I didn't! Why won't anyone believe me?" Matthew crossed his arms defiantly.

Sofia shut her eyes for a moment. She reminded herself that Matthew was only an exuberant, impulsive little boy. "You had them in your hands, Matthew. It was a natural conclusion."

"You mean like that man saying you threatened him?" Matthew asked.

"Yeah, like that, Matthew." She put her arm around him. "It looks as if we both have some explaining to do and some fences to mend, huh?"

"I was just watching some big kids, Mom. Suddenly, they

started to run. One of them said, 'Here, Matthew. Hold these.'"

"He called you by name? Then you must know him. Who was it?"

Matthew shook his head vehemently. "You know what happens to kids who tell on other kids. They are ostriches."

"You mean *ostracized*?"

"Yeah, that."

Sofia tousled his hair. "Matthew, doing the right thing is not always easy, but it is the best way. Besides, we have two months until school. Everyone will have forgotten all about it."

"I hope so," Matthew said.

Sofia frowned. Matthew had said the boy was older. Was he afraid that someday he would be attending the same school? "Think about it, Matthew. Your actions have consequences for more than just you." She kissed him on the forehead. "We'll talk with Officer Quimby tomorrow—together."

She turned out the light and closed the door. She believed that Matthew would do the right thing because she and Jim had always led by example. If somehow they'd failed, there was more than their liability for damages at stake here.

Sofia needed to think about something else. Maybe the pink quilt square. Discovering that the central square had belonged to the famous Mona Lisa had for a time clouded her appreciation of the heirloom as a whole. Not every square represented someone as famous, but the contributors had endured incredible challenges and not only survived but thrived. Just as the individual blocks sewn together made a strong whole cloth, her ancestors' DNA building blocks made her the person she was today. That made it more important to her than the fame.

Her computer chimed, pulling Sofia from thoughts about the quilt. *Who is emailing at this time of night?* Bryce had apparently texted his mother, because the email was from Gina, who expressed concern that Bryce could be linked to their problems and hurt his father's chance for reelection.

Sofia gritted her teeth. She pushed the Caps Lock key to capitalize the letters and wrote: *MATTHEW DIDN'T DO IT. NEITHER DID I!* She hit Send and shut off the computer. She could empathize with Matthew.

The next morning, she and Officer Quimby agreed that Matthew might be more forthcoming away from the station. She invited him for lunch to put all of them at ease. But first, she wanted to see the shop in daylight and with a clear mind.

Sofia was surprised to see Marla and Julie already dressed in paint-stained jeans and T-shirts. "Surprise!" Julie shouted. "Look!" Three walls in the outer room were clear of soot.

"The butcher paper kept the smoke from them," Marla said. "That leaves only the ceilings, common wall, and kitchen to wash and repaint if we need to."

"What about your jobs?" Sofia said.

"I took the day off," Julie said, "and Marla can stay until noon. We took photos before we touched anything in case the insurance agent needs them, and we didn't touch the common wall."

Sofia tied a scarf around her hair. "You two are the best friends anyone could ask for." Then she asked, "Did one of you set the bucket and brush on the counter?" She remembered putting them in the closet herself.

"Maybe the firefighters did," Marla suggested. But Sofia could think of no reason why they would.

Sofia decided to start with cleaning the ceiling. By eleven she had the ceiling, except for the section inside the closet, free of soot. Stepping inside the closet, she noticed that the ceiling tiles there were askew. *I need to get Jim to take a look at that*, she thought. She was startled when the alarm on her watch chimed as a reminder of her appointment to meet with Officer Quimby.

Marla had left for work, and Julie was soaping the window. After hurrying home to shower and change, Sofia had just set the table when the doorbell rang. She called Matthew to come downstairs as she opened the door for Officer Quimby. "Let's eat first," she suggested. "I have gazpacho and chicken salad sandwiches with yellow squash chips. Is herbal tea okay?"

"Yes ma'am," he replied. "That sounds real nice." He greeted Matthew, offering a handshake. "Are you looking forward to the celebration?"

"I guess," Matthew answered with a shrug.

"Well, everyone's busy, so it's just us," Sofia said, trying to make light of the situation.

The officer's deadpan expression and his lack of chatter during lunch seemed ominous. As it turned out, she was right.

He set his napkin by his plate and cleared his throat. Sofia braced herself for bad news. "Mrs. Parker, there's a problem."

Chicago, Illinois
Summer 1867

Anxiety tasted like metal in Hannah's mouth. The moment was here. To make Carlton Vanhiller trust her out of his sight, she needed to rob people. But that would make her a criminal too. Would the police understand that it was the alternative to death? Why should they believe her? Hannah realized that her choices were few: Remain under Vanhiller's rule and be a thief, or break away and risk recapture, even death. If she escaped, the police were liable to arrest her.

"Have you ridden a train, Hannah?" Vanhiller's voice intruded.

"Never. I have listened to the whistles calling in the night and dreamed I was on the train, going as far away as I could go."

"It is only to the next depot and then back before any donor is the wiser."

"Will you be with me?"

"Nearby, my dear, watching." Vanhiller rubbed the top of the snake head with his thumb as he spoke.

She struggled to wipe the revulsion from her expression and smiled up at him. At least she would be outside this prison. Two nights here and she was already unsure of herself. What must it be like for the others, who had been so long under his influence?

Vanhiller handed her a book. It was Hawthorne's *The Scarlet Letter*. "I have read it," Hannah said.

Vanhiller threw his head back, laughing. "Open it."

The pages had been hollowed out, leaving only a narrow border. She hid the red-hot rage she felt at the destruction of a book. "I don't understand."

Tapping the book with his cane, he said, "It makes the perfect jewelry box—for someone else's jewels. There may be Pinks lurking about. The first thing they do is look in your handbag and open the parasol. But the book is a new wrinkle I came up with."

Hannah's pulse quickened at the thought of Pinkerton detectives on the same train. If she could contact them, they might be a bit more forgiving than the police. "That's so clever of you, Carlton." She affected exaggerated admiration.

He offered his arm and she smiled, slipping her arm into his. When they left the building, she inhaled the warm August morning air. *Outside . . . step one.*

At the station, Hannah and Vanhiller blended into the crowds milling around the waiting area. A freckle-faced street urchin pushed through the clusters of people, pausing to tug at men's coattails and shove newspapers at them. Holding a copy high, he shouted in a high-pitched lisp, "Get your papers here! *Dock Workers Threaten Strike!*"

Hannah sucked in her breath. Just above the fold was a headline in bold black: *Body Washes Ashore!* Could it be Lily?

Vanhiller's eyes steadily focused on her. She dared not indicate that she cared about anything or anyone but the theft and the donor. "Can we go on the platform, Carlton? I've never seen a train up close before."

"Patience, my dear. You'll need a ticket to board. Stand here; don't move."

Hannah stood frozen in place, her head swiveling as she scanned the packed quarters for someone who might help. Where were the uniformed police she had anticipated? Could they possibly be dressed as passengers? *Undercover.* She remembered that was what it was called. She saw a gentleman in a dark suit carrying a small satchel. Was he looking for pickpockets, or only for his lady? She turned in time to see Iris slip her hand into a woman's open handbag and retrieve a gold compact.

She jumped at the firm grip on her arm. "You wanted to see the locomotive up close, did you not?" Vanhiller guided her from the waiting area to the platform. Hannah stood awestruck. The locomotive was so much bigger than she had imagined, and the black metal was so polished that she saw her reflection. Wisps of steam hissed and swirled and quickly evaporated. Vanhiller smiled. "Look around you. There are so many eager contributors today."

Hannah forced a light giggle. Aware of Vanhiller's tight grip on her arm, she scanned the crowd for someone who could help.

"Board!" a man in a dark blue uniform with shiny brass buttons called. "All aboard!" More people poured onto the platform, brushing past Hannah and stepping into the cars. Most of them seemed so relaxed, as if they took trains all the time.

Hannah hesitated, glancing toward the locomotive and the dark curl of smoke rising from its stack.

"Board!"

"Go," Vanhiller told her. "I'll be watching. You may not see me, but I'll be there."

Of course he wouldn't want to be associated with her in the event she was caught. Her first thought was to board through one door and hurry right out the next until she saw Lucas standing among the crowd, staring in her direction. She had at least two pairs of eyes on her.

She dismissed any thought of bolting—at least, not at the station. Her time would come, just not yet.

"Climb aboard," Vanhiller told her. "Take a seat until the train is underway. Do not approach a donor until we are outside the city."

She nodded and climbed the steps to the passenger car. Hannah took a seat on the aisle near the rear of the first car. A slightly bent, gray-haired woman in a dove-gray travel suit took an aisle seat across from her. On her lapel, a diamond swan pin flashed brightly as she moved. She wore a diamond bracelet that winked at the edge of her gray gloves. The veil on her simple hat was heavy, like a mourning veil, and tied under her chin. Hannah found the woman fascinating, perhaps because she looked as out of place on the train as Hannah felt.

The woman carried no parasol, which was almost a fashion requirement in Chicago, especially for someone so elegantly dressed. She clutched her ebony leather purse protectively in her lap. It appeared heavier than one would expect. Hannah thought that odd. If she flaunted the diamonds, what was in the purse that was more important to her?

The locomotive gave a loud *whuff* and then another; the wheels screeched against the rails. The bell clanged and the whistle signaled. Hannah grabbed the seat back in front of her to steady herself as the car lurched forward. Sooty smoke floated through the open windows as the train gathered momentum.

She coughed, tasting soot. Away from the station, the air inside the car cleared, and Hannah settled back to study the passengers, all potential "donors," as Vanhiller called them. Some read their newspapers; a few were writing with difficulty as the car rocked and swayed. Several well-dressed men spread playing cards across a flat suitcase between them. None suspected that they could lose their valuables at any moment.

Hannah understood that Vanhiller was somewhere in this crowded train car, his cold eyes watching her. Perhaps Lucas was seated forward, even though she couldn't see him. She thought about making her way to the exit and leaping from the train. She'd be injured for sure; after all, the train was going at the horrific speed of thirty miles per hour. They were in open country now. Where would she go? That seemed like a plan of last resort.

If Vanhiller was correct, there were Pinkerton undercover detectives on board. She turned her head so the woman in the expensive-looking gray suit was in her peripheral vision. Hannah was aware that the woman's eyes shifted focus around the car. She watched the people, not the scenery. Could she be the one called the Chameleon? If she was wrong, Vanhiller would no doubt seize her, and she'd have her turn in the "thinking room."

Hannah prided herself on her ability to notice things that others did not. She was intrigued by the obvious weight of the purse the woman carried. Could it hold a weapon, badge, and handcuffs? The woman was dressed and carried herself like an older woman. Yet Hannah was sure that the veil hid a more youthful face. She thought she glimpsed an unwrinkled neck. Could her gray hair be a wig?

If she was correct in her assessment, this woman was a Pinkerton undercover detective. Hannah said a silent prayer as the woman stood and turned toward the rear door of the car. It was a natural move, as the water closets and the food car were at the rear, just in front of the baggage car. Hannah followed her.

The woman opened the door. The metal-on-metal noise and the creaking of the swaying cars took Hannah by surprise. She paused briefly as the woman stepped into the next car and held the door for her.

Hannah knew she had to act fast, before Vanhiller could follow. She pretended a fainting spell as he had instructed her, grabbing the woman's wrist and nearly crumpling to the floor. She moaned weakly.

A strong, firm grip clamped on her hand, and a second hand slid around her waist. Although Hannah had expected the show of strength if she had guessed correctly, it startled her. "Please," she whispered softly, "he's watching. Help me."

Hannah held her breath. She had made her move. She no longer controlled what would happen now.

8

Cabot Falls, Vermont
Present Day

"Mrs. Parker, Mr. Norton is claiming that you deliberately set the shop fire because of an argument. He wants to press charges. He said he has eyewitnesses that you threatened him."

Sofia's jaw slacked as she tried to comprehend what he was saying. She knew Norton was a cranky and miserable person, but accusing her of arson was just ludicrous. "I-I told him that nothing in life is free. I merely meant that when you try to harm others, it's liable to come around to bite you. That's all. I am not a vengeful person, Officer Quimby."

"Yes ma'am. I don't get the feeling that you are. But you two have a history: Mr. Norton got a court order to stop the boys from building a tree house, and he filed that injunction to keep Matthew from opening a lemonade stand. There's a lot of bickering between the two of you. Arguments can start small and escalate to serious business."

"It's all one-sided! I am flabbergasted that you'd think—"

Officer Quimby held up his hand. "Oh, I'm just telling you what the records show. I can't argue that he's not a troublemaker, but there is evidence that the fire started on your side of the common wall."

Sofia took a deep breath to regain her calm. "Surely he doesn't hold me responsible for bad wiring."

"I do all the forensics work since I took those courses at Quantico," Officer Quimby said. "I don't get much practice at it here, so I'm not the defining word, but from what I saw at the scene, it looked like it was deliberately set. I have asked my friend from Montpelier to take a look at it."

Sofia tapped the table with her finger. "Well, there is something you should know. When I left the shop before the fire, I put away my cleaning supplies, including a bucket and brush, in the closet. After the fire, the bucket and brush were sitting on the cabinet. Tell me how that happened unless someone was in there after I left. If it was arson, it was someone else."

Officer Quimby pulled out his notebook. "I'm checking who else had keys. So far, it seems just you and the Andersons, who are out of town. I will keep looking, Mrs. Parker." His mouth curled in a tight smile. "If I don't come up with the right answers, I'll answer to our old English teacher." He referred to Pat Cooper, Sofia's neighbor, who had taught generations of high school students.

Sofia couldn't even pretend to smile. She was worried. It was impossible to prove a negative. How could she prove she hadn't committed arson? How could Matthew prove he had not used fireworks and started the fire? She trusted the officer to do his best, but to prove they had done nothing wrong, she needed to find out who had.

Officer Quimby turned to Matthew. "I think looking through the high school yearbook is a good idea, Matthew. If you see the boy who handed you the matches and fireworks, I'll talk to him. Usually people just need to be asked the right question. Of course, if you know the boy but just don't want to tell me . . ."

The front door swung open, and Luke and Bryce came in. "The paper's here," Luke said. "It has a picture of the fire, Mom. Oh, uh, Officer Quimby . . . hello, sir. Sorry, Mom."

"That's all right. Bring it here, Luke. Officer, this is Bryce McCray, my sister Gina's son."

Nodding toward Bryce, Officer Quimby shoved his chair back. "I'd better get back to work. Thank you for lunch, Mrs. Parker. And Matt, I look forward to hearing from you, okay?"

Matthew shrugged, and when Sofia nudged him with her elbow, he said, "Yes sir."

When Officer Quimby had left, Sofia opened the newspaper. Above the fold were two photos of the fire: one with the flames showing bright against the night sky, and the other, the ruins left by the fire.

Below the fold were photos of the construction on the green before the fire. Sofia squinted at the figures in one photo. Several people were kneeling and appeared to have things in their hands, although it was unclear. She couldn't see the features of one figure some distance away, but she had washed that T-shirt so many times that she would have recognized the leaping ninja on white anywhere. It was Matthew, and he was far away from the kneeling figures. Could those be bottle rockets in their hands?

Sofia leaned back in her chair, smiling. "Boys, tomorrow we will take a field trip to the newspaper office. I'm about to blow something up. A photo, that is."

If she was right, she was about to put one accusation to rest. But how was she ever going to convince Norton that she had had no part in the fire? Better yet, how could she convince the authorities?

Chicago, Illinois
Summer 1867

Whatever happened next, the die was cast. Hannah winced

at the firm grip on her arm. This was either an extremely strong old woman or a young woman in disguise. If it was the latter, then she was either a thief or, as Hannah hoped, one of the Pinkerton detectives hired to protect passengers against the pickpockets. Hannah moaned weakly, "Oh, I think I'm going to faint."

She held her breath. If this was the detective, would she give her away, arrest her, or play out the illusion?

"Oh, you poor girl!" The woman's voice was wobbly and strained. "Here, let me help you to the powder room. I'll bathe your face. You'll be just fine."

Doubt flooded Hannah's thoughts. What if she had guessed wrong? What if this woman wouldn't—couldn't—help?

"In here, dear girl," the woman said. And in one swift motion, she set Hannah on the fainting couch in the small enclosure and snapped handcuffs around her wrists. Her voice changed, as did her posture. In that instant, she became a vibrant younger woman. "Now, who is watching you, and who are you?"

"Are you the one they call the Chameleon?" Hannah whispered. She kept her gaze on the entrance. Could he be standing there, listening?

The woman paused. "I must be getting careless," she mumbled. "Call me Kate." She pulled a brass badge from her handbag.

"I knew it—Kate Warne, head of the female detective bureau!" Hannah said. "My name is Hannah Reed, and I'm in danger. All of us are at risk, forced to steal for Carlton Vanhiller. Help me. Help us! Please."

The woman released the veil from her face and tucked it over her hat brim. Recovering her composure, Kate asked, "What's the situation?" Her steel-blue eyes focused on Hannah's.

Hannah took a deep breath and blurted out her story. "I feel sure that Carlton killed my friend Betsy. And now Lily is missing. I'm so frightened. I just can't steal from people. Please arrest him."

The woman shook her head. "I am afraid that I can't."

"Then arrest me," Hannah pleaded.

"What do you think would happen? He'd pay your way out. Then you'd either be exactly where you are now—or worse. We need proof. You will have to go back as if nothing has happened."

Gasping, Hannah grabbed the woman's arms. "I can't! Don't you see? If I don't take him money and jewelry, he will put me in that dark closet and starve me. I'm afraid!"

"If I arrest this man now with no evidence but your word, it won't help. The other women may not back up your accusations."

"They are as afraid of him as I am," Hannah said.

Kate patted her hand sympathetically. "They depend on Carlton for survival. Over a period of time, that makes for a very strong bond. Survival is a strong urge. We allow our minds to play tricks to achieve that. He probably reminds them that they owe the victims nothing. When they hear that long enough, they come to believe it."

Hannah shook her head. "I won't."

The detective smiled sadly. "I was twenty-three when my husband died. I might have been just like those women."

"Not you!" Hannah cried out. "And not me."

"Perhaps we are stronger, more determined. I was lucky. Allan Pinkerton was willing to give me a chance. I was able to bluff my way into a traditionally men-only domain. Now there are quite a few women detectives."

"Are you ladies all right in there?"

Hannah grabbed Kate's sleeve. "It's Carlton!" she whispered.

In her imitation of an older voice, Kate called out, "Yes, thank you. She's coming around. Just a few minutes more, and the young lady will be right as rain." She turned back to Hannah. "You, too, will find your strength, Hannah. Think like a detective, not his chattel."

Hannah didn't want to believe that the other women felt beholden to Vanhiller.

"Without proof of murders, Vanhiller would be charged only with receiving stolen goods, nothing more. Did the missing women have identifiable items he might have kept?"

Hannah snapped her fingers. "Yes! Betsy Day had an aquamarine ring with her initials inside it. And she wore a gold band on a ribbon around her neck. It was engraved: *R.T. & E.D. 03/05/1840.* Those were the initials of her deceased parents and their wedding date."

"Items like that are more difficult to sell or pawn. Find a reason to be about the house." Kate pulled the diamond pin from her lapel and removed the bracelet. "Here. This will prove that you were working on his behalf in here. You must go back. You won't be there long, I promise. And one of us won't be far away from you. What can you do to signal?"

Hannah remembered the upstairs shades. "The shades upstairs in front are always closed. I will raise one of them." She stuffed the jewelry inside the book. "I must go. Carlton will be suspicious."

The woman veiled her face again, resumed her stooped posture, and opened the door. Vanhiller stood in the corridor. He glanced briefly at the woman, and Hannah was sure he saw that her pin was missing from her lapel. He smiled and tipped his hat. "Is the young lady all right?"

The detective acknowledged him with a slight dip of the head. "Yes yes, I believe it was just a touch of the vapors. She tells me this is her first train ride. I'm sure she was just a little anxious."

"Allow me to return her to her seat, ma'am." He steered Hannah back toward the original car. "Nice job," he whispered when they reached her seat. "Ma'am?" he said loudly and tipped his hat. "If I may be of further assistance . . ."

"Thank you. I am quite all right now," Hannah replied. She fingered the book that held the jewelry. This was a trivial amount of "donations" for the day. Autumn had been put in the thinking room when she had much more. Could she do as the detective wanted? Could she locate any evidence that would prove Vanhiller responsible for the disappearances—and possibly the murders—of women he took in?

Hannah reviewed the list of residents there. She dismissed Millie and the brother, Lucas, immediately. Iris seemed a lost cause; she delighted in thievery.

Perhaps Cadence or Autumn had not lost hope or identity. Kate was correct, though. Vanhiller had so cowed the other women because they depended on him for their very lives. She needed an ally on the inside.

The train slowed; they were pulling into a depot. Vanhiller had said to detrain at the first stop, and they would work the station and return to Chicago before evening.

The inbound train was already on the second track. Hannah left the train and milled about the crowd waiting to board for Chicago. Lucas stood at the entrance in case she tried to leave. She had not yet earned his trust.

Vanhiller pressed a ticket into her hand. "When we reach the Chicago depot, you must exit immediately before anyone notices they have donated to the Vanhiller home for indigent women." He gave Hannah a wicked grin.

Hannah joined in his mirth, although her first reaction was to break away screaming, to beg the detective not to send her back. She nodded and boarded. Looking about, she didn't see Kate among the crowd of passengers. Had she changed disguises or continued on the first train? The woman had asked her to return to the house of horrors. Get evidence, she'd said. And then she'd left Hannah to her own devices? How was this helping?

Sighing, Hannah took a seat just as a large, gregarious man ambled clumsily down the aisle and staggered into her seat back.

He tipped his hat and mumbled an apology before pushing on to the next car. Hannah stared at her lap. Nestled between her book and handbag were two men's gold watches and a wallet thick with cash. How . . .?

That man! He had to be a Pinkerton detective. Kate must have had him deliver enough "donations" to keep Vanhiller satisfied. Kate had kept her word. Hannah relaxed. She was safe—for now. She could concentrate on what she must do to get the proof that Vanhiller or his brother was a murderer.

She needed to search the house. Hannah realized that she needed to convince the Vanhillers that she was trustworthy enough to freely roam the house. Hannah knew that she was about to embark on a dangerous mission, and she didn't know the rules. She realized that a great deal depended on her alone.

9

Cabot Falls, Vermont
Present Day

Sofia had made an appointment to meet the photographer at the newspaper office. Jim had planned to go with them, but he had gotten a fire call during the night and had not yet returned home. She left the girls to prepare lunch and took the boys with her. "The first thing you'll be asked to do when school starts is write an essay on what you did this summer, right? Well, now you'll have something pretty exciting to write about," she told them as she pulled into a parking space outside the one-story building.

The photographer met them at the reception desk. "I'm Delores Adams," she said, shaking hands with each of them. "Call me Dee. I understand that you're interested in one of the photos we have from the day of the fire. Follow me."

She led them through a large room with desks and computers and huddles of people. "It's a lot busier than usual for a weekly," Dee explained, "but Cabot Falls is suddenly plunged into a crisis, and we're scrambling to get all the facts."

Alarmed, Sofia frowned. She'd been concentrating on her own problems so much that she hadn't followed the local news. "What do you mean by a crisis?" She hadn't talked with Jim, realizing he'd been busy after the fire call. "Are you talking about the arson? What happened?"

"'You haven't heard?" Dee asked. "The arsonist had

concentrated on abandoned buildings. Then two residences burned last night. Fortunately, they were empty and for sale, but it's an escalation that's making everyone nervous. Added to the arson problem, there's the bigger problem with Grand Point that popped up overnight."

Sofia realized that Matthew had paused, captivated by the pandemonium in the newsroom. She grabbed his hand and followed Dee.

Dee laughed. "Pretty neat, huh, Matthew?" She paused before continuing. "As I was saying, we're still trying to get the facts straight, but the city attorney for Grand Point served an injunction to stop Cabot Falls Inn from building the new wing. They claim that the inn is already partially over the line of incorporation and they want a share of the tax money. Construction on the new wing has to stop until it's all settled."

Sofia shook her head. "And Sam thought his little bet with the Grand Point mayor was going to be a simple good-natured rivalry with nothing more at stake than a little humiliation. But isn't there some sort of grandfather clause to protect the village?"

"Our researcher is looking for old deeds and court records, and of course the mayor's office is scrambling for answers. But so much was lost when the courthouse burned. We'll see." Dee stopped at a door with a printed sign: Do not enter when light is flashing. "Here we are."

She turned on a light box and laid the filmstrips against it. "So much of our stuff is digital now, but we got these from a citizen who happened to be in the right place at the right time with his Kodak. The photos are in sequence with some before and some after the fire. Which ones were you interested in?"

Sofia studied the negatives with a small magnifier. "That one, the third from the left, the one with the view of the booths before the fire started, and the next one, where the flames are just beginning to show. But I'm really interested in those boys in the foreground."

"Oh, the focus is on the booths, and the depth of field is not that good. The part you want will be blurry probably, but I can try to bring them up." She closed the door and flipped a switch. The tungsten light went off, and the room took on a red hue. Sofia and the boys moved with her to a tall instrument, where she put the film in a holder and slid it into the top of the enlarger. "Most people have moved completely to digital," she explained, "but I still like to use film and a good old-fashioned darkroom now and again." She flipped on a switch and a fuzzy version of the picture appeared against the easel on the table. Flipping off the enlarger, she next put a piece of stiff white paper in the easel beneath the lens. Again she flipped a switch, exposing the paper with the image.

"It's blank!" Matthew said after the photographer switched off the enlarger again. "It didn't take."

Dee picked up the paper by its edges. "It's magic time, Matthew. Watch this." She dipped the paper with tongs into a foul-smelling solution, and seconds later, the picture appeared. "Now it goes in this bath to stop the process," Dee said, "and then into the fixer—uh, the preservative." The image appeared on the photographic paper and then was moved to the next chemical baths. "Watch yourselves. This next step is really hot." She laid the photo facedown on a shiny flat surface and pulled a cover over it to keep it flat. Then she repeated the process for the second photo.

After a few minutes, she flipped the tungsten light back on and showed them the pictures. The first photo showed the kneeling boys, with Matthew standing about ten feet away. The second photo showed the boys running in Matthew's direction. He was still standing in his original spot.

"I'm sort of fuzzy," Matthew said. "But I can tell it's me, because that's my ninja shirt."

"Does it help?" Dee asked.

"It does show that Matthew was nowhere near them, and there is no visible fire. This must be moments before the fire started. I just wish the boys' faces were clearer, but thank you for trying," Sofia said, trying to keep the disappointment from her voice.

She was anxious to return home to see if Jim was all right. Two fires in one night and at least one every night for days had to be taking a toll on the volunteers. And Jim was a math teacher, for goodness' sake. He was healthy and strong, but he certainly wasn't used to such continuous, strenuous work. Besides, she missed his calm, logical support. She wondered if the police were any closer to finding the arsonist.

As they threaded their way back through the desks in the newsroom, Sofia spotted a familiar figure. Norton was seated at one of the desks with a balding older man, probably a reporter. That had to mean more trouble. And it was most likely aimed directly at her.

As if on cue, her cell phone rang. It was Officer Quimby. "The arson investigator from Montpelier is here, Mrs. Parker. Can you meet us at the shop this afternoon around three? I think you need to be there."

Sofia wondered if she should pack a toothbrush, or if the jail furnished them. She compressed her lips in a thin line of determination.

Chicago, Illinois
Summer 1867

Hannah determinedly walked up the steps of the Vanhiller

home. She could feel her blood rushing through her temples like a dull roar in her ears. She had been so close to freedom a few hours earlier, only to have the Pinkerton detective, Kate Warne, tell her she must go back or the monster Vanhiller would be free to hunt her down and continue his reign of terror on indigent women.

His grip on her arm was firm and unyielding as he half-guided, half-pushed her into the house. He'd said not two words to her since they'd left the train depot. Was he angry because she had remained in the powder room too long? Did he suspect that she was conspiring with a Pinkerton operative?

"I am disappointed in you, Hannah," Vanhiller said as he hung his derby on the hall rack. He guided her down the hall and into the workroom. "You didn't even attempt to collect any donations on the return trip."

Hannah's shoulders relaxed as the tension of anxiety drained. So that was it. He suspected her only of not picking pockets. "I did work. I guess you just didn't notice me." She smiled as she dumped the jewelry, watches, and wallet the detectives had secreted to her. "I had hoped you'd be pleased with me."

Surprise was reflected in Vanhiller's face as the items tumbled onto the bench. "I . . . I'm flabbergasted, Hannah. You did a wonderful job. You are swiftly becoming my star pupil."

Hannah unpinned her hat. She decided to play to his need for control. "I am glad that you are pleased. May I wash up now? I didn't realize that train travel could be so gritty."

"Yes yes, my dear. The others will be returning with Millie soon. Wash up and then come back down if you want to."

"Thank you, Carlton. I could start supper, if you wish. I helped in the kitchen a good deal at the orphanage, so I'm sure I can help Millie out since she was supervising the others today." *Supervising*, she thought, nearly laughing at her choice of words.

Vanhiller had again drafted Millie for guard duty since he'd had Lucas help him watch her all day.

Hannah hurried upstairs and put away the hat and handbag. She washed her face and then rushed downstairs to the kitchen. The others would be home soon. She put a quart of water on the range and measured out four cups of rice when it came to a boil, lowering the fire beneath it and covering the pot. She retrieved the leftover vegetables and several already-cooked chicken thighs, deboning them and cutting the meat into small cubes. From her kitchen duty at the orphanage, she had learned to stretch meager amounts into meals for a large number of people.

She hummed loudly as she opened every drawer in the kitchen and checked the cabinets for evidence, carefully replacing things as she found them when she heard the others returning.

Millie stopped short at the door to the kitchen, her face reflecting dismay at finding someone else in her greasy little oasis from Vanhiller.

Hannah invoked Vanhiller's name as she folded the other ingredients into the fluffed rice. "Carlton thought it would be nice if I helped you out, Millie, since you were gone all day. I hope that is all right with you."

Millie let her breath out in slow motion and acknowledged Hannah with a quick nod. She snatched her apron from the hook and seemed at a loss as to what to do next.

It was difficult to tell if she had won Millie over with her help or frightened her. Millie was probably terrified of being expendable, and who could blame her? To Vanhiller, all of the women were no more than tools of his trade, to be discarded when they became useless in his eyes.

"You work so hard, Millie. I don't mind helping at all. At the orphanage I helped cook, did the dishes, dusted, and did quite a bit of the housework."

Millie's smile was more of a grimace. "It is hard doing everything myself." It was the first time Millie had spoken in Hannah's presence. She had no sooner spoken than she swiveled her head as if making sure that Vanhiller was not within earshot.

Autumn was missing from the table again. *How much longer can she go on taking Carlton's punishment of starvation in that hot, dark storage spot under the stairs?* Hannah wondered. She had to get evidence—and fast.

"I'll help with the dishes, Millie," Hannah said after supper. She turned and smiled at Vanhiller. "That is, if it's all right with you, Carlton."

Preening his mustache, he returned her smile. "Of course, my dear. Your performance today was outstanding." He turned toward Iris. "I believe that you have some real competition."

Hannah ignored the glower Iris shot her and gathered up the plates and silverware, then carried them to the sink.

Millie slipped the gold band from her finger and placed it on the windowsill before she added water from the kettle to the sink. Hannah stood next to her, drying the silverware as she set it aside. Hannah could see that the inside of the band was not smooth; perhaps it was engraved. She needed to see what it said. "Millie, was that Carlton calling you?"

Millie quickly grabbed one end of the dish towel and wiped her hands before rushing from the room to find Vanhiller.

Hannah snatched the ring from the sill and held it so that the engraving was clearly visible by gaslight. Her heart thumped against her rib cage as she read it: *R.T. & E.D. 03/05/1848.* "Oh, Betsy," Hannah whimpered. "It is true. You really are dead." She dared not let the tears come. She realized that they would seal her own fate.

Recovering quickly, she returned the band to the sill just before the kitchen door swung open and Millie reentered, scowling.

"No? I guess I'm just hearing things, Millie. Shall I take the trash out?" She reached for the bin, but Millie grabbed her arm.

"No! That's Lucas's job." Millie's voice was firmer than Hannah had thought possible. The backyard was forbidden, apparently. *Why?* She noticed there was no key in the door slot. Hannah thought perhaps one key controlled both exits—and the Vanhillers controlled the key.

"I'll put the rest of the food away, Millie," Hannah suggested. "You've had a long day."

Millie looked at odds. She paused as if trying to decide if it was all right to indulge herself just this once. She relaxed, untying her apron and rehanging it. "Thanks," she mumbled and then darted from the room.

Hannah quickly spooned some of the rice mixture into a napkin and placed the remainder in the icebox. She exited the kitchen and walked into the hall, stooping to slide the napkin under the door. "Autumn, are you all right?"

"Thank you. Be careful. You are taking a chance doing this." Autumn's reply sounded weak. "I don't know how much longer I can hold on."

"Don't give up," Hannah whispered. "Please." She dared not tell her why. She didn't know if Autumn might be desperate enough to inform on her to please Vanhiller.

"Hannah, what are you doing?" Lucas asked, coming around the corner.

Flinching, Hannah replied, "I picked up a pebble in my shoe. I'm all right now. I'm going upstairs with the others." Hannah knew what she had to do, and tonight was the night.

She joined the other women, who were already in their nightgowns. The moment she was inside, Lucas slammed the door to the room and slid the bolt closed. Hannah changed in the low light and slid under the sheet, staring at Lily's empty cot. If she didn't end this soon, that cot would be occupied by another unsuspecting woman or even a young girl like Iris.

She lay on her cot, clutching the pink quilt to her. *Mother, why did you do this to me? Look what you have done.* Hannah shook off the thought. No, she had done this to herself by acting before she thought. Perhaps her mother had done her a favor. Without loving, helpful hands to guide her, she had become strong and determined. The detective had asked quite a lot of her. But she knew that she could do it.

Hannah waited until she felt sure that the others had fallen asleep. She sat up, listening for the slow, even breathing. No one stirred. Slowly, she tiptoed to the window and noiselessly pulled up one of the shades. With no gaslights in the neighborhood, the houses across the street were only silhouettes in shades of gray to black. Did any of those residents wonder about this house? Weren't they even curious? Perhaps Vanhiller had told the neighbors it was a boardinghouse for ladies. Maybe people were just too busy with their own lives and problems to notice or care that things were not right here.

A lone pedestrian in a top hat stumbled slowly along on the other side of the street, singing at the top of his voice:

". . . Whispering voices on accent meet; mmm . . . sparkling eyes of woman fair . . ."

The voice trailed off, and the man was gone. Hannah cocked her head, listening. Was he a Pinkerton, checking on her as Kate had promised? They were certainly experts at disguises if the situation called for them. Or had he been only as what appeared: a man who had indulged himself too much and was happily making his way home? She worried that she was counting on them too much.

If they didn't come through for her, then she would do it on her own, even if she had to take her chances that the police might arrest her. *I can do this.* She had almost convinced herself.

She looked up at the sky. The moon was no more than a thin smile tonight, but the stars were glorious. The North Star and the Big Dipper and its miniature companion sparkled like diamonds against black velvet. How many times had she sat at the orphanage window and wished upon the evening star that her life would be different? This was not what she'd had in mind.

Hannah crept back to bed. She only hoped the signal would be noticed.

10

Cabot Falls, Vermont,
Present Day

*S*ofia noticed that Luke was unusually quiet as she drove them home from the newspaper office. He'd been tight-lipped ever since he had looked at the photos, and she could see him in the rearview mirror, staring at them now.

She pulled to a stop at the signal. Watching him in the mirror, she said, "Luke? Do you have something to say?"

His head jerked up as she called his name. "Uh, no ma'am . . . well, maybe. I'm thinking."

The light changed and she made a left turn toward home. Sofia had a feeling that Luke was holding something back. She mentally debated with herself: Should she press him to tell her, or should she trust that he would not withhold information that could clear his brother? The latter argument won—for now.

"*Tutto è bene che riesce bene*. Nonna used to tell us that when things looked the bleakest," Sofia said as she pulled into their driveway. "It means that 'All is well that ends well.' Nonna firmly believed that if we do our best, things will turn out okay."

She couldn't comprehend why Norton saw her as the enemy, unless it was her close proximity at the shop and home. Maybe he was one of those people who could never blame himself for anything and she had become his designated scapegoat. He had rebuffed her every attempt to be a good neighbor. She could only imagine what tales he had told the newspaper reporter today.

Jim's car was in the drive, and he greeted them at the kitchen door. "Do I smell like smoke?" he asked as he leaned over to kiss Sofia. "I showered twice at the station, but I still think that I smell smoke."

"The photographer said there were two fires last night," Sofia said as she returned his kiss. "You must be exhausted."

"Yeah, I ache all over. I never thought it'd be this busy for summer. I sure hope they find the arsonist soon."

"These were empty houses?" Sofia asked.

"Yes. They both had For Sale signs. That Mark Keeler fellow is sure having a bad run. Both houses were listed with his agency," Jim said.

"Mark Keeler? Isn't he the one who helped the mayor get us the shop free? Tough break," Sofia said as the family sat down to lunch.

Vanessa and Wynter had made cold cucumber soup and tuna sandwiches. The sandwich platter had no sooner been passed among them than Luke excused himself. Sofia heard the back door open and close and looked up in time to see Luke riding off on his bicycle. The photos were not on the kitchen counter. She sighed wearily. *Il cuor non sbaglia*, as Nonna would say. *Trust your instincts.* And her instincts were that Luke had thought through whatever was on his mind and made the right decision.

They were eating strawberry gelato for dessert when Luke strode in, smiling confidently. "You're off the hook, ninja boy," he told Matthew as he slid into his chair and pulled his plate to him. "I know the photo was fuzzy, but I recognized Billy Ray Brown and his brother, Robert. I just explained to them that my little brother wasn't going to take the blame for something they did."

"Thanks, Luke!" Matthew yelled. "Thank you, thank you, thank you!"

"Just don't let it go to your head, squirt," Luke said, laughing.

Bryce burst into a wide grin. "This family is so cool, Aunt Sofia. I wish . . . I wish I could stay all summer. This is so fun."

Sofia squeezed his hand. "I wish you could too, Bryce. We'd love to have you." She wondered what Gina would think if she saw her buttoned-up son wearing his shirttail out and cutoff jeans, and hiding his curls under a cap that said *Rock Rocks*. She surely couldn't miss that big grin, though.

"Luke, do you think the boys will actually turn themselves in?" she asked.

"I waited while they called their dad. He's a lawyer, so he'll go with them." He turned to Matthew. "You know them, Matthew. Why didn't you say anything?"

Matthew shrugged. "They're your friends, Luke."

"I thought they were friends. I guess we'll just have to see when school starts," Luke said. He gave Matthew a light tap on the arm.

Sofia winked at Jim. She couldn't help but be proud of the way Luke had handled the situation. And he had done it without any coaxing. He had certainly inherited some of the special traits that Hannah Reed demonstrated, if Marla's research was accurate. She didn't believe that the diary would have mentioned her along with the pink square unless she was an ancestor. But where did she fit in? Why couldn't they find Hannah's parents, and what did she have to do with the initials A.J.? If only things weren't so weird right now, she would have loved to concentrate on the research.

Enough of the past; she needed to deal with the present. Encouraged by Luke's success in ferreting out the boys responsible for the fire, she decided she'd try to talk some sense into Norton one more time. Somehow she had to break through that hard shell of anger.

Sofia checked the time. "Kids, I have to meet Officer Quimby and the fire investigator at the shop. Don't go too far, and be sure to lock up, okay?"

"I'm going with you," Jim said.

"You aren't too tired after battling fires all night?" Sofia asked. "I don't mind doing this alone."

"I have every confidence that you could handle it alone, sweetheart, but we're in this together."

Relieved to have the emotional support, she grabbed her keys off the hook. "I'm sure it was just faulty wiring," Sofia said. In truth, she wasn't sure about anything anymore.

Chicago, Illinois
Summer 1867

Hannah wasn't sure if she'd done the right thing as she lay on her cot, listening for any sound that told her that rescue was imminent: footsteps scraping on the porch, a pounding on the door, shouts of "Open up in the name of the law." But dawn came, and she was forced to acknowledge that she was still at the mercy of the Vanhillers.

Iris sat up and threw off her sheet. "Why is that shade up? Carlton doesn't like it when people can see in. Who did this?"

"I-I guess I forgot to close it last night," Hannah replied. "I couldn't sleep, so I watched the stars until I felt drowsy."

"Well, close it. Lucas will be unlocking the door any minute, and he must not see it open."

Cadence stirred. Autumn's cot was still empty. She was confined in the "thinking room." Hannah hoped that would be over soon. She knew Iris was right. Lucas would surely notice that the room was brighter than usual. She hurried to the window, pausing only briefly to check the street for any activity, and pulled the shade down as she heard the bolt slide open. Where could the Pinkertons be? Kate had said to signal with the open shade if she found proof. Why weren't they here, arresting Vanhiller? Had they noticed the signal? Had they even looked? Hannah tried to calm herself. She realized that her fear of abandonment was deep-seated and difficult to shake.

Subdued by disappointment, she joined the others at breakfast, resigned to another day of reluctant thievery under the watchful eye of one or more of the Vanhillers. The deeper into this ring of pickpockets she was, the more difficult it would be to convince anyone of her innocence. She felt a rush of anger at Kate Warne. Her lips compressed into a thin, determined line. If she was on her own, so be it. Today she would take the first chance she got to get away. Someone had to believe her. Perhaps she should go to one of the newspapers. Wouldn't they jump at such sensationalism as captive women forced to rob or die?

"Hannah."

Her head jerked at the sound of her name. "Sorry, you were saying . . . ?"

Vanhiller smiled. "I said the others are waiting. Be alert, dear girl. Daydreaming will get you caught."

Hannah nodded and followed Vanhiller to the door, standing aside with the others as he unlocked the door. She watched as he slipped the key back into his breast pocket. On the ride to the depot, she swiveled in her seat, hoping to spot any sign of a Pinkerton following them or standing along the way.

"Why are you so fidgety?" Iris asked. "Stop it. It's annoying."

At the station, Hannah sought out the powder room, stalling so that she didn't have to steal from anyone. Perhaps she could escape through a window before Vanhiller sent one of the others to check on her. A woman in a stylish rose silk dress and a billed hat with a dark veil and pink roses on top primped her golden hair at the mirror. She turned as Hannah entered and put her fingers to her lips in a warning of silence.

Hannah sucked in her breath. It was Kate Warne wearing a blond wig.

The detective motioned for Hannah to join her at the window away from the door. "You signaled. You have proof already? What did you find?"

Nodding, Hannah said, "The ring Millie wears belonged to Betsy Day. It bears the engraving I told you about on the train. I saw it with my own eyes last night when she took it off to do dishes. Are you going to arrest him? He's in the depot."

"It only makes her in possession of stolen goods and a suspect in the disappearance of Betsy Day. But it gives us a reason to search the home and property and take them into custody when we happen onto evidence of illegal captivity and identifiable stolen goods. That gives us enough time to do a thorough investigation and uncover the truth."

Kate patted Hannah's hand reassuringly. "The Vanhillers and the other women are scattered about now. We will wait until tonight when everyone is there. Are there any weapons that you are aware of?"

"I don't know," Hannah replied. "Carlton is never without that lethal-looking cane, but I don't know about the others. It's possible that Lucas carries a weapon, but I think they count on his size and the ability to manipulate him into doing what Carlton wants."

"We'll have the warrant by this evening. Open your handbag," Kate instructed. She emptied the contents of a bag into it. "This is enough loot to satisfy Vanhiller meanwhile. Expect us to arrest you too. In case we don't find more evidence to hold the Vanhillers, he won't know that you were the one who turned them in."

Hannah roamed about the depot, mingling with crowds but thankful that she had the "loot," as Kate called it, already stashed. It would keep her out of the "thinking room" so that she could lift the key from Millie and unlock the door for the Pinkertons. The front door was solid oak. The effort it would take to break through it would give the Vanhillers time to get weapons or be prepared for fight or flight. If the door were unlocked, it would simplify matters a great deal.

She was relieved when the day had finally passed and they had eaten. Hannah volunteered to do dishes with Millie again, and when they were done, she said, "Here, Millie, let me remove your apron for you. It seems to have developed a knot." Pretending to struggle to release it, she easily lifted the key from Millie's pocket. Now if the woman just didn't notice . . .

Exiting the kitchen, Hannah saw that the corridor between the kitchen and front door was empty. She slipped off her shoes and crept noiselessly toward the door, carefully slipping the key into the slot. She sucked in her breath as its click seemed magnified in the silence. Done.

"Hannah! What are you doing?" It was Vanhiller.

She stood frozen in place, her mouth gaping open as she saw in the low light that he had yanked the snake head from the cane. The glint of metal left no doubt that the carved snake head was in reality the handle of a dagger. She screamed as he grabbed her arm and pulled her to him.

As he jerked her from the door, it burst open, and a rush of men with weapons drawn suddenly filled the corridor. Vanhiller dropped the knife and held his hands in the air, a look of shock on his face. A burly red-haired man with a well-trimmed beard yelled orders in a distinctive Scottish accent at the others as he pulled Vanhiller's hands from the air and handcuffed him. The men shouted and peeled off in different directions. Some rushed into the downstairs rooms and others ran up the stairs. No doubt startled by the sudden activity, the other women shrieked and screamed.

It all happened so fast that Hannah stood with her hand over her mouth, unable to speak. She could only nod numbly when Kate stepped in and asked, "Are you all right?"

She recovered enough to reassure Autumn and Cadence as they were led down the stairs and out with Vanhiller, Millie, and Lucas. "It's going to be all right. Don't be scared. We're safe."

Kate handcuffed Hannah as if she, too, was being taken to the precinct, but released her when the others were out of sight. Hannah's breath was no longer labored and choppy. She smiled at the detective, who had kept her promise. "What happens now?"

"We'll gather the evidence to make a case against them. I'm sorry to say, though, that the operatives discovered evidence of graves in the backyard, and one of them appears fresh. I'm afraid that you are correct that your friend is dead, and probably Lily too. The good news is that just that alone is enough to give the Vanhillers the noose."

Tears welled in Hannah's eyes and splashed down her cheeks. "I thought as much. If only—"

"Think of the women who will never be their victims because of you, Hannah." It was the man with the Scottish accent who spoke. He introduced himself as Allan Pinkerton. "This was a good night's work. The police will take care of them from now on."

"What will happen to the women?" Hannah asked. "They are victims too."

Pinkerton nodded. "We'll help the older women locate relatives or perhaps get help from the charities until they are able to function on their own. Iris is another problem." He shook his head sadly. "We'll see."

"I guess I knew that. It just makes me feel so bad," Hannah admitted. She let out her breath in a long wheeze. "Can I be a Pinkerton?"

The man threw back his head in a loud laugh. "You are only just beginning, young lady, with a long way to go. But somehow I think you have it in you to succeed. Kate is certainly impressed, and I trust her judgment implicitly." He turned to Kate. "Set her up in a room-and-board house, my treat until she earns a check."

Kate nodded. "What about Robert?" She looked to Hannah. "Robert Pinkerton heads the New York office and handles the finances. He questions all our expenditures."

"She is a material witness we need to protect. When Stanton hears how Hannah helped bring down the worst ring of pickpockets ever to frustrate his company, he'll be happy to finance her stay. List it as an investment in the future." He smiled at Hannah. "Because that's what she is."

For the first time since leaving the orphanage, Hannah spent a night free of fear at a boardinghouse, eating a full meal in the dining room and delighting in the people of varying ages who treated her with genuine respect.

Kate boarded there too, and the next morning, she escorted Hannah to the Pinkerton headquarters. The imposing sign with the enormous painted eye and the slogan *We Never Sleep* jutted over the sidewalk as assurance to the innocent and a warning to criminals.

"I can hardly wait to get started," Hannah said. "What do I do first?"

"First, you listen, and you learn," Kate said. "You'll receive a stipend while you train in the needed skills. When you qualify, you will get a generous income, because make no mistake: It is dangerous work."

Hannah soon discovered that "listen" and "learn" meant months of grueling training, not just in laws, handling firearms, and overt investigation, but in disguising herself in a variety of personalities and ethnicities, and changing her voice and inflection. Christmas and New Year's Day passed, and she wondered at some of the odd things Kate taught her. She leaned to sashay like a flirtatious girl and carry herself with the haughty pride of a dowager noblewoman. She learned to waltz and to serve tea, to affect an uneducated backstreet accent and to swagger—"cocky," Kate called it. Her repertoire of personalities grew, and still she was not ready, Kate told her.

As the weeks passed, Kate continued to fill her in about the Vanhillers, giving her more understanding about the nature of people. Hannah learned that as a child, Lucas had taken the blame and the beatings to save his younger brother, which explained Vanhiller's gentle treatment toward him. Their loyalty stemmed from the secret they shared: that one day Vanhiller had taken their father's snake-head cane and ended the abuse once and for all. The fugitive brothers had fled Philadelphia and, somewhere along the way to Chicago, had rescued Millie from a similar situation. The three of them were locked together forever in their conspiracy. Apparently their own sad lives had done nothing to ingrain empathy in them for anyone else.

"You'll learn quite a lot on the job," Kate reminded her, "so don't feel bad if you don't do everything correctly at first. It takes time and practice. Create as many characters to play as you are comfortable with, and only if you are comfortable with them. Look around the boardinghouse. You'll see those you can emulate. Make disguises easy for you, but never stray too far from the truth, or you could get confused about what you told a subject. I choose names that are close to mine: Katherine, Katie, Kathy. The last thing you want is to not answer to your pseudonym."

Hannah nodded. Names like Anna, Anne, and Annie came to mind. The initials on the pink quilt flashed through her mind. She had retrieved it back from evidence, and it now stretched across her bed at the boardinghouse. It taunted her, teased her with its secrets. Perhaps with her newfound knowledge of investigating, she would eventually find the mother who had left her. For now, she needed to shove everything from her mind but work.

"Are you with me, Hannah?" Kate asked. "You seem far away. This is not the time to drift. Today is special."

"Special?" Hannah asked.

"Here you are, and congratulations." Kate smiled at her.

Hannah stared at her hand. It was a shiny new Pinkerton badge. "You mean—?"

"You are now officially a Pinkerton."

"And I get an assignment?" Hannah asked, excitement making her heart pick up speed.

Kate laughed. "Your first assignment is to ride the train and arrest pickpockets."

Hannah burst out laughing. In a few short months, she had gone full circle from being a pickpocket to catching them. Her mood sobered when Kate handed her the handcuffs and a weapon. It was serious business, protecting the railroad passengers. Pickpockets were not dangerous for the most part. But a new trend was developing as the rails stretched toward the West Coast through less civilized territories.

Robbers had become so bold that they actually boarded the trains in isolated areas and robbed the passengers at gunpoint before disappearing into the hills. They even stole the mail, looking for cash. The small Secret Service Bureau didn't have enough agents to handle the increase in these thefts, and the government had drafted the Pinkerton Agency to fill the void.

"I'll work hard at whatever task you assign me," Hannah told Allan Pinkerton when he came to congratulate her, "but I hope you'll keep me in mind for one of those assignments." Chicago and all of the cities were so crowded now. Hannah had gone from the overcrowded orphanage to the dormitory as a captive of Vanhiller's and now to a small room at the heavily populated boardinghouse. The open territories she read about sounded magnetic.

"I'm delighted that you want to prove yourself, Hannah," Detective Pinkerton told her. "But you would be on your own, far away from our help if you needed us."

"I can do this," Hannah insisted. She only hoped that she was right.

11

Cabot Falls, Vermont
Present Day

Sofia hoped she was right—that it was faulty wiring. The alternatives were too scary. When she arrived at the shop, she was surprised to see a small crowd. In addition to Officer Quimby and Fire Inspector Darcie O'Leary, she saw that Mark Keeler, the mayor, and Norton were there. She was so grateful that Jim had insisted on coming.

Inspector O'Leary told them to wait outside. Eventually she motioned for Officer Quimby to join her, and the two of them disappeared into the kitchen.

Outside, the mayor said, "I regret getting you two into this, Sofia. I'm getting pressure to withdraw our support."

Astounded, Sofia gasped. "Sam, I've already purchased the supplies. I—"

Sam held up his hand. "Now, I didn't say that I was caving in, Sofia. Norton even started a petition to close you down. Some of the shop owners here have signed it."

Before Sofia could protest, Inspector O'Leary invited them in. "I've determined that it is arson," she said. "At first glance, it looks like it started at the fuse box, but it's an amateur attempt, and a botched one at that. I'll take a sample of the residue back to the lab. I should have it identified in a few days. When Officer Quimby told me that you said items were removed from the closet, I stopped at the village planning department to look at the original building plans. New structures require firewalls that extend into the attic. This is an old structure—no firewalls, and they have a common attic."

"That opens up the suspect list to every shop owner then, doesn't it?" Sofia asked.

"Not exactly. I spent the morning checking the other accesses. Most owners didn't know about them and had simply painted over them, sealing them. It's only a matter of time before we figure out which one of the openings was used," the inspector said. "And why."

Sofia had mixed feelings about the new information. She was glad that at least some of the suspicion was off her. She hoped that would quell the movement to close her down. She hoped it calmed down Norton too. He was certainly a lot quieter now.

She shook hands with the investigator. "Thanks, Inspector. It felt terrible with fingers pointed at me."

"It only proves that the trap door in your closet was accessed. Ryan will dust it for prints, but unless the arsonist is on file or they catch him red-handed and he confesses to the rest . . ." She shrugged. "Or maybe he used gloves."

A balding man stuck his head through the door. Sofia recognized him as the one who had been talking to Norton the previous day at the newspaper office. "Hello! Kerry Watts, *Cabot Falls Community News*. May I have a moment of your time?"

Sofia motioned for him to come inside, anxious for him to get the news out about the inspector's findings.

When she had repeated the new information, Watts thanked her. "But the shop owners only own their businesses, not the actual shops. The strip is part of the estate of the Cabot family, and they are as big a mystery as the fires."

"How so, Mr. Watts?"

"This branch of the Cabot family had few male heirs, so the name eventually disappeared. We're trying to track through marriages to find descendants, but it's tedious work. The lawyer administering the estate trust says the estate includes most of the downtown property, including the property these shops are on, the green and the adjacent property, and the Cabot Falls Inn. But he refused to talk about descendants. Seems fishy, doesn't it? Well, back to the salt mines. Thank you, Mrs. Parker."

Sofia locked up, and she and Jim got in the Suburban. Sofia went to turn the key but instead turned to Jim with a puzzled look.

"I keep wondering who would benefit from a fire here, Jim. The business owners gain nothing if the building burns. This whole row of shops could have been lost if someone hadn't spotted the fire early. Isn't that lucky?"

Jim shrugged. "I wonder if luck had anything to do with it."

"What are you saying?"

"Maybe we ought to listen to the tape of the call that came in to the station and see if the caller is recognizable. What do you say?"

"Let's do it now. And then we need to get that wall up, and we'll be finished except for bringing in the bistro tables and getting the food set up. Poor Jessop Norton has all that ruined equipment to deal with. I'm thinking maybe we should go help him when we're finished," Sofia said.

Jim grimaced, shaking his head vigorously. "I know it's your nature to want to help everyone, but are you sure you want to do that? He's been nothing but trouble, and who knows how he'll react? I think it's a bad idea. Besides, who's to say that he didn't start the fire himself, hoping that it would be blamed on the arsonist? Who's to say that he isn't the arsonist? What do we really know about him, anyway?"

Sofia started the engine. Jim might be right, although it seemed preposterous. This was made to look like a natural fire to cover up arson. How crazy was that? What would be Norton's motive? She knew she'd feel better if she tried to help him. But right now, she felt numb.

Chicago, Illinois
January 1868

Hannah felt numb. She was only vaguely aware that the January chill had permeated the heavy wool cape she had wrapped around her arms. In Graceland Cemetery, she stood at the graveside of Kate Warne, the woman who had not only saved her from Vanhiller but had also trained her to be a Pinkerton detective. She felt as if her heart had been ripped from her chest. In no more than four months, Kate had become her best friend and mentor.

And then, in less than a month's time, she had become ill and died from pneumonia. As illogical as Hannah knew it was, she felt as if once more she had been abandoned.

Allan Pinkerton sighed wearily. "She succeeded far beyond my utmost expectations. Mrs. Warne never let me down."

"I don't want to ever let you down either," Hannah told him. "I still had so much to learn from her."

"Kate trained you well in the time she had, Hannah. She had confidence in your ability to sort through the most minuscule clues and come to the correct conclusion. She thought you were the most resourceful of all her trainees. But you are so young. You have so much more to learn."

She nodded her understanding. She hadn't experienced the world outside the orphanage enough. She hadn't learned how to see through the false faces people offered. "Watch the eyes," Kate had instructed her. "They tell us more than words. Even their posture tells us what they won't say. Do they cross their arms as if to shut you out? Do they look you in the eyes or turn away? Listen to their voices get shriller as they lie."

Mr. Pinkerton took over most of her guidance thereafter, although he kept her on the pickpocket detail for several more months. She was aboard the swaying trains so much that walking on solid land seemed strange. On her few days off, she visited Whiteside and read to the girls, or she sat in her boardinghouse room staring at the initials and the puzzling string of letters on the pink quilt, curious about her phantom mother. She had asked herself a dozen times if she was afraid of what she might find. Why else did she balk at the most burning question in her mind?

Three years after Kate's death, Hannah stood outside Mr. Pinkerton's office. She inhaled deeply, sighed visibly, and rapped on the closed door. "I came here in 1867, Mr. Pinkerton. It is now January 1870. I can't change my age but one day at a time. But I'm twenty now. I feel I have earned a chance at better assignments," she told him. She braced herself for his resistance.

Allan stroked his auburn beard and gazed at the ceiling as if absorbing what she'd said. "All right, Hannah. I need you in Missouri immediately. A lockbox with diamonds worth thousands was stolen at gunpoint from one of Stanton's trains. He promised safe delivery, and it's up to us—you—to recover them. Otherwise, he's out thousands of dollars, and our reputation will be severely tarnished.

"The perpetrator is already in jail, but he refuses to reveal the location of the diamonds. Do what you have to do to get them back. Your wardrobe and essentials along with details are waiting for you at the station. Godspeed, Hannah."

Hannah's thoughts reeled; she hadn't expected an assignment quite that quickly. It was a job Kate would have performed. Hers were difficult shoes to fill. Of all his female detectives, Hannah was probably the tallest at five foot seven. Her figure was more slender too. Had Allan already planned on sending her on this assignment? Once she had a look at the wardrobe he said waited for her, she would know for sure. *Allan Pinkerton is a sly old fox,* Hannah decided as her carriage pulled up in front of the train depot.

In the sleeping car, she removed her hat, and when she was sure no one was observing, she rechecked her weapon and returned it to her handbag with her badge and handcuffs. She set the bag on the seat next to her. Extracting the file that the agency had sent ahead of her, she read the particulars. Erasmus Jones was convicted of the diamond theft based on the testimony of the baggage car employee. But he refused to divulge the whereabouts of the diamonds, even for a reduced sentence. If the diamonds remained missing, the rail company would be liable for the loss, which Stanton considered devastating. Allan took great pride in the Pinkertons not only getting the culprits but also recovering stolen goods.

Jones was married to a Maude Jones, who had moved into a hotel near the prison so she could visit him every day.

Kate had taught Hannah to always blend into any situation and to be as empathetic as possible to win trust. If Mrs. Jones had moved near her husband and visited often, Hannah thought that was the way to reach her. Upon arriving at the Independence depot, Hannah ordered her bags sent to the hotel where Mrs. Jones was

The Thief of Hearts **107**

staying. When the dining room opened for the evening, she had the hostess point her out.

Hannah took a deep breath and approached the table. "Hello. I noticed that you are alone. I am too, and I hate to eat alone. Do you mind?" She slid into a seat opposite the woman before she could say no.

She knew not to rush things or look too anxious. "I'm Anna Reid. And you are . . . ?"

"Maude Jones."

She waited until the soup, a creamy potato with tiny bits of cheese sprinkled on top, arrived. When she had taken a few spoonsful, she said, "I find this town awfully noisy, don't you?"

When Maude had agreed, Hannah said, "I won't be here long. I'm just here to visit my dear husband. I'm embarrassed to tell you, but he's in the prison here. I hope to visit him a few times before I return to Pittsburgh."

Maude's eyes widened. "My husband too! That's why I'm here. We could go together tomorrow."

The next day, the two had rolls and coffee together and then hired a carriage to the prison. As soon as Maude had been admitted to the visitors' area, Hannah returned to the hotel and stayed out of sight there until that evening. She casually mentioned to Maude that her husband seemed agitated. "He said that one of the prisoners whose name he didn't know was bragging that he knew where there were diamonds for the taking because he heard another prisoner talking in his sleep."

Maude's eyes widened and her hand trembled. She set down her teacup.

Hannah knew she had her full attention and continued concocting her tale. "He said the man boasted that he would be released first and would get the diamonds before the other man got out. That just seems so wrong, don't you think?"

Maude frowned. "I . . . I don't feel well. I'm going to retire early." She reminded Hannah of a bird flushed from the weeds as she fluttered and bumped her way through the dense arrangement of tables and chairs to exit the dining room.

Hannah smiled to herself when Maude had disappeared up the stairs. The trap was set. The next morning, all she had to do was follow Maude and recover the diamonds once she retrieved them. Later, she telegraphed Pinkerton headquarters:

MOUSE TOOK CHEESE STOP CAT HAS MOUSE STOP.

It was a simple case of a little deception winning over greed. Mr. Stanton would be pleased.

Hannah personally handed the lockbox to the clerk in the baggage car and waited for him to sign the receipt and stow the box in the safe that was bolted to the floor of the baggage car. Short of another train robbery—and what were the odds of that?—the case was all over but the paperwork. "No one knows these are on board," Hannah told the clerk. "Let's keep it that way."

The train to Chicago was crowded, and Hannah took her seat. She hurriedly completed her reports and opened the book she'd purchased at the bookshop near the hotel: *Little Women* by Louisa May Alcott. She planned to give it to the girls at the orphanage, but for now, Meg, Jo, Beth, and Amy March would keep her company on the ride back to Chicago.

The expected peaceful ride home took a sudden turn for the

worse when a loud, muffled voice shouted, "Hands in the air, passengers! This is a holdup!"

Hannah could feel the blood drain from her face before rage took hold and turned it red-hot. She was right in the middle of a train robbery, and the only weapon near her was *Little Women*. Her flush of success in recovering the diamonds vanished as she chastised herself for letting her guard down. She had been so full of her triumph that she'd put her tools of the trade an arm's length away on the other seat.

A few women screamed, and men cursed and muttered protests. As her resolve increased, her lips tightened into a thin line of defiance. Hannah swiveled her head enough to see two men wearing bandanas over the lower parts of their faces.

"Make no sudden moves," one of the men instructed. He wore a brown shirt and dark breeches with black boots. *Useless information*, Hannah reminded herself. *People change their clothes.* She concentrated on things he couldn't change. *Height: approximately five feet ten. Posture: one shoulder slightly lower than the other, perhaps from an old injury—gunshot wound? Hands: broad, with stubby fingers. Veining on his hands that of a man past forty.* He was lanky, and the gun belt around his hips was black leather, with decorative tooling of distinctive buffalo heads.

Hannah turned back around and, as cautiously as she could, slowly advanced her hand toward her handbag.

"I wouldn't do that if I were you, miss," the second man said.

She let out her ragged breath in a wheeze.

"Now hand over your valuables, please, ma'am." His voice was almost soothing, as if he were talking to a child, reassuring her that everything would be fine.

Hannah's mind flashed on the contents of her handbag: badge, handcuffs, and weapon with her roll of bills. Would he shoot her when he realized he had a Pinkerton at his mercy? "No!" She was surprised at the force in her voice.

Above his bandana, his green eyes flickered in a show of amusement, further infuriating Hannah. "No?" he asked.

She was sure that beneath that kerchief, he was smiling. "No!" Hannah repeated. At the same time, she was thinking, *This one is taller. Around six feet one. He has broad shoulders. His hands are those of a younger man, not yet thirty. His skin is olive.* As he leaned past her and reached for her handbag, she gasped audibly and grabbed his arm, which she noticed was taut with muscle. "Please, let me."

The other man was halfway down the aisle by now, his hat upside down to hold the valuables the passengers dropped in. He looked back. "Trouble?"

The younger man raised an eyebrow. "Is there?" he asked Hannah quietly. She slowly shook her head. "No trouble," he called out. "You go for the safe. There's plenty more there." Now he took her arm. "Ma'am, if you'll come with me, please? And I'll take that necklace."

Instinctively, her hand covered the locket. "Please . . . It's the only . . ." Her shoulders sagged, and she reached back and unhooked it.

He removed his hat, releasing a shock of dark curls that matched the ebony strands curling up around his earlobe.

Glaring at him, Hannah dropped her necklace into the hat. Bitterly she fought back the tears that threatened to appear. That necklace and the quilt were all she had of the life she didn't know. It served only to make her resolve more firmly than ever to find the mother who had abandoned her. She looked him square in the eyes. "You will pay for this." She thought her heart would break at that moment. Reluctantly, she rose to her feet at his insistence.

With a firm hand on her arm, he guided her down the aisle in front of him. Glancing out the window, she saw five horses, one with an empty saddle. The second man was already off the train and back on horseback. That meant this one was alone, but his weapon was still drawn. At the exit door, he said, "Your money, ma'am? Thank you."

Tight-lipped, she slid the top along the drawstring to make as small an opening as she could and reached in to retrieve the small roll of bills. Her hand touched her weapon, and for a brief moment, she considered her options. With his weapon out and at the ready, she realized it would be foolish to try anything. She shoved the money into his hand. "Here!"

He motioned for her to open the door and step onto the small platform between the two cars. The masked man leading the horse with an empty saddle had no trouble keeping up with the slow-moving train.

"Thank you, ma'am," the man said. "You've been very helpful."

As he prepared to jump, Hannah snatched the bandana from his face. Momentarily startled, he quickly recovered and leaned toward her. His lips brushed hers before he leaped off, rolled on the flat ground, leaped up, and mounted the horse in one fluid motion.

Still clutching the bandana, she shook her fist in the air and called out, "I won't forget this!" Dumbfounded by his boldness, she self-consciously touched her lips. The bandana still held a faint odor of peppermint. *How dare he!* Yet the hint of a smile played across her lips. Had that been an attempt to kiss her? The door opened. "Are you all right, miss?"

"Shaken a bit, but yes, I'm all right." She returned to her seat and reached into her handbag to retrieve her notepad and pencil. She wanted to jot down everything she could remember before any details were corrupted by input from the others. She figured she'd never live this down at headquarters. How they would tease her!

As she reached for the pencil, her fingers brushed against something in her handbag. It was her necklace. He had somehow surreptitiously dropped it into her bag. *How intriguing.* Perhaps he could tell from her reaction that it meant so much to her. He might still have a sense of decency in him. Too bad she would eventually have to place him under arrest.

12

Cabot Falls, Vermont
Present Day

"What if we can't do it?" Sofia asked Jim as she parked curbside at the fire station. "What if we can't recognize the voice?"

"Then they will find the arsonist without our help," he said as they went inside.

Fire Chief Benson, the only paid firefighter, looked up from his desk. He stood and shook hands with Sofia. "You here for a tour, or are you rescuing us with some delicious muffins, perhaps?"

"Sorry, Chief, I didn't know we were coming until the last minute. But I promise to bring you a batch soon," she said.

"We'd like to listen to the tape of the call the night of the shop fire," Jim told him. "We're hoping we might recognize the caller."

Sofia and Jim sat down while the chief cued the tape. The voice was muffled and distorted, probably deliberately. It sounded the same on all the calls they listened to. That would be too coincidental. It was probably the arsonist. The fires seemed almost perfectly timed to start as the others were under control, the chief reminded them. "I sure hope that fire inspector from Montpelier can shed some light on it."

"She's already made some interesting discoveries about the shop fire," Jim told him. He filled him in, then added, "She'll probably drop by here when she's finished with all the loose ends."

"Chief, you and the volunteers got to the shops pretty quickly, didn't you?" Sofia asked. "I mean, if you hadn't, there would have been a lot more damage."

"Yeah, there were already a few civilians watching. We had to get them to move their vehicles so we could get closer. I took a few photos of the early arrivals for the record," the chief said. "I haven't uploaded them yet."

"They'll be on our website?" Jim asked.

"Yeah. Have you been to bed since last night's fire?" Chief Benson asked. "You look pretty wiped out. Better get some rest, Parker. Who knows what tonight will bring?"

As they drove home, Sofia said, "The chief is right, you know. You need at least a nap. If the arsonist strikes again tonight, you don't want to start out tired."

Jim yawned as if on cue. "When I volunteered to replace summer vacationers, I never thought it'd be this strenuous or that I'd have to give up coaching Matthew's Little League baseball this summer."

"Oh, I don't think Matthew is upset. He's pretty proud of you. I am too." She turned from the main street toward home. "I'll take you home and then go by the library. There's something the reporter said that I need to ask Marla about."

She had a feeling that finding the arsonist and learning about the absentee Cabot descendants were somehow connected. They were like squares in the quilt. Each piece was interesting alone but would be far more valuable when pieced together to make a whole picture. She smiled. Was it possible that her Hannah Reed detective gene was kicking in? Wouldn't it be interesting if she solved the case before Officer Quimby and Inspector O'Leary?

It was tempting to blame it all on Norton. He and the fires had seemed to arrive at the same time, and he was the most disagreeable man she'd ever met, throwing around accusations without any evidence to back them up. Of course, she could understand it. The fire had started on her side of the wall, and they didn't really know each other. Too, the damage to his shop was so much worse. She was fortunate that she hadn't brought in a lot of equipment. His exercise machines were a total loss before they had ever been used. For his sake, she hoped that he had full insurance coverage.

With Jim off to nap, she headed for the library. She was surprised to find Chief Benson there when she arrived. He was at the desk speaking with Marla, who directed him to the local history section and then squeezed Sofia's hand. "Hello, friend. How did the inspection go?"

"It was arson all right. And someone went to a lot of trouble to set it on my side. Did you know that all of the shops have a common attic?"

"I guess I never thought about it," Marla said. "But I did notice that they have no sprinkler systems. I guess back when they were built, there was no such thing. But having a common attic should make one easy to install. And I'm betting that the council will make sure the owners do."

"Speaking of owners, did you know that the shops and all the surrounding land belong to the Cabot estate? The Cabot Inn too," Sofia told her. "The reporter I talked to said that he hasn't found a single Cabot heir."

Marla checked out a book for another patron and then said, "I know. Money from the estate is mostly dispensed to charitable institutions, and it keeps the community college expanding. The early Cabots had a few sons, but thereafter, it was pretty much girls, so that the Cabot name disappeared as they married. The one cousin that the mayor was counting on to open the celebration turned out to be a con man. He's wanted for fraud in New Hampshire, and apparently he got a new identity, because he's disappeared."

"That's a shock. I wonder where he wound up," Sofia said. "I'm sure that our illustrious mayor will be able to spin it in a way that most of the townspeople will be none the wiser. He's so intense about this Founder's Day celebration. Not so much that he's going to help us get the shop ready, though. Jim will put up the drywall tomorrow morning. It should be ready to paint by afternoon, barring any more trouble."

"What more could happen?" Marla asked as she stamped and handed a book to a patron.

Sofia sighed wistfully. "There's an old Italian saying that Nonna used to quote: *Chi male comincia, peggio finisce.* It means a bad beginning makes a bad ending."

She just hoped she wasn't correct.

Chicago, Illinois
Summer 1871

Hannah had been correct about the teasing. She was the brunt of many a joke when she returned to headquarters. She took a deep breath and turned the knob on Allan Pinkerton's office door. "You wanted to see me?"

"Sit down, Miss Reed." His chair squeaked as Mr. Pinkerton leaned back and looked off into space for a moment.

Hannah swallowed hard. "Sir, if you'll just let me explain . . ."

He leaned forward and picked up a paper. "Oh, Miss Reed, I just wanted to ask you about the details of the robbery."

The tension drained from her shoulders, and Hannah relaxed. "They must have boarded when the engineer throttled down to make the curve."

Mr. Pinkerton nodded. "I see. It's this description, Miss Reed. You say the younger man lost his bandana and he revealed a 'Romanesque nose and strong jawline with what might be chronic stubble.' You described his eyebrows as 'brooding' and his eyes as emerald with dark flecks 'like shadows on the water.'" He leaned back. "Miss Reed, it sounds more like a romance novel than a crime report. Is there something you're not telling me?"

Hannah flushed. Had she really said all that? "I wanted to be thorough in my description." She dropped her hands, palms up, into her lap. Had she really written those words?

"Why do you think he gave the necklace back to you?" Mr. Pinkerton asked her. As his eyes met hers, she flinched under his intense gaze.

"I don't know. Maybe a good instinct overcame a bad one." She squirmed in the chair. He was asking questions she didn't want to ask herself.

Pinkerton slammed his fist on his desk. "These gangs are a menace to travelers—and to the rail companies. They steal the mail, looking for cash. They have overwhelmed the sorely undermanned Secret Service. The companies want our help."

"And I want to be a part of that, sir." The sting of having people robbed right under her nose made her determined. "When the two robbers jumped the train, they rode off toward the hills." Hannah balled her fists. "I'd like to go after them."

Pinkerton's expression was one of bemusement. "Do you ride, Miss Reed?"

"As in horses, sir?" She'd never been any closer to a horse than she dared. They were so big and intimidating. "I understand the concept, sir. Get on and stay on."

Mr. Pinkerton muffled a laugh behind a closed fist, turning it into a cough. "Miss Reed, you said firing a weapon was a concept of point and shoot. We vividly remember how that turned out."

Hannah wished she knew how to stop a blush as she recalled the memory of her first encounter with a shotgun, a requirement for every Pinkerton regardless of whether they ever used one. So eager to prove herself, she had fired unprepared. It had thrown her backward, and she'd landed—hard—on her bottom. The bruise on her shoulder from the stock eventually faded, but the memory had not.

She laughed lightly, hoping to cover her embarrassment. "I'll figure it out." There was no way she was going to let a little wariness about that huge beast keep her from finding the man the passengers called the Gentleman Bandit. She made a guttural harrumphing sound deep in her throat.

The next day, Hannah stood watching nervously as her instructor led a bay mare toward her. "This is Country," he said. "She's a real lady."

Hannah stood frozen as the massive creature touched her cheek with its nose. It was soft, like the finest kid glove. She tentatively reached out a hand, and when Country didn't object, she traced the white blaze that stretched the length of the mare's head with her finger. Country's ears flicked and rotated.

"Good job," the instructor said.

Hannah wasn't sure if he was talking to her or the horse.

"Now stroke her neck. Let her know that she can trust you."

Moments later, she sat atop Country, a long way from the ground. The instructor led Country into a fenced area. By the end of her session, Hannah felt adequate in the saddle while Country trotted around the circle. She reported as much to Mr. Pinkerton when she returned to headquarters.

"I'm ready to go after him . . . them," she told her boss.

"Miss Reed, something else has come up. I need you for an undercover assignment. Don't worry about the gang that robbed your train. A posse of Secret Service, the local sheriff, and a couple of our own tracked them down in the hills. It ended in a shootout, so there won't be a need for a trial. Fortunately, the diamonds were recovered by a Secret Service agent."

Hannah felt a sharp, stabbing pain in her heart. So the Gentleman Bandit was no more, leaving only the ghost of his brief touch. She would not smell peppermint without remembering him.

It was bad enough that she had allowed herself to be robbed. Oh, the teasing she had endured! Could she ever redeem herself in the eyes of her fellow detectives? But in her most vengeful dreams, she had never expected it to end with him dead. She clasped her fingers together, waiting for the details of her assignment.

"A gang known as the Apple Gang blocked the train tracks with what seemed to be a herd of obstinate cows. What the engineer didn't know was that while he waited for the cowboys to herd them to the other side, the gang had relieved the soldier guarding the military payroll at the rear of the train of the money. He said he was overwhelmed. The cash was in a canvas bag clearly marked *Property of U.S. Treasury* with the destination tag of the U.S. Army."

Hannah grimaced. The Youngers, James, and now Apple gangs—criminals got bolder as they joined together. Journalists turned them into folk heroes. It made it harder to stop them. "You said undercover, Mr. Pinkerton. Who am I this time?"

"We've set you up as Harmonee Rich, a popular singer from back East. We printed fake newspaper articles and a few posters advertising shows that never happened. It'll be convincing."

Hannah burst out laughing. "Mr. Pinkerton, the only singing I've ever done is lullabies to poor captive babies at the orphanage. Why can't I be a schoolmarm or—"

"Where you're going, they have no need for schoolmarms, but they are hungry for entertainment. Trust me, they won't know if you can sing. And they won't care. But if you're not up to it . . ."

There was no way she'd turn down an assignment. She'd just have to trust Mr. Pinkerton that her singing was no problem. When she returned from this one, there would still be the matter of the pink quilt with the strange initials.

As a Pinkerton pretending to be different people, she had strengthened her curiosity about her true identity. Who was this mother who had left her to an orphanage with nothing but a locket and a quilt? She had faced down criminals; she could face down this woman. "When do I leave?" Hannah asked.

"Immediately. You will take the train to the town of Dry Gulch, Montana. Don't look for it on the map. You won't find it. It's a ragged little town with both good and questionable people. Most of them depend on Fort Grimm for protection and their livelihood. Dry Gulch is a rest stop for those heading West. Be careful, Miss Reed. You're still a bit green, and you may not always know the bad guys from the good ones out there." He laughed. "There should be a law that the bad guys must wear black hats."

Hannah's lips compressed. "Kate trained me well, Mr. Pinkerton. I can still hear her voice in my head. I won't fail." She sincerely hoped that her bravado was not just bluster.

Aboard the train on the way to Montana, Hannah learned that a replacement payroll for the fort was aboard the same train. It would be a long, tedious trip with miles of rail, and there would be many places where another robbery could occur. Hannah made her way back to the baggage car.

Finding the door between the dining car and the baggage car unlocked, Hannah felt a flash of anger. She readied her weapon and pinned her badge so it was clearly visible on her shoulder. Pushing in, she startled the guard, who was sprawled in a chair, talking to the clerk. His shotgun was on a rack out of his reach. Both men scrambled to their feet, staring openmouthed.

"From now on, you will keep this door secured. You will not open it without proper identification, and you will keep your weapon at the end of your arm," she snapped. "Is any of that unclear?"

"Yes ma'am. I mean, no ma'am. Sorry, ma'am."

"Any further blunders and I will have you replaced at the next whistle-stop," Hannah said. "Now lock the door behind me." Her skirt billowed as she whirled toward the door and stormed out. She replaced her badge and weapon in her bag. At her seat, she kept her bag on her lap. *Once burned . . .* Hannah couldn't remember the rest of the proverb, but she knew she was ready this time for anything.

At least she thought she was. Days later, she stepped from the train onto the rickety platform at Dry Gulch. If there had ever been a bush or prairie grass here, it had dried up and blown away long ago. She quickly opened her lace parasol, her only defense against the intense heat, and scanned the scene.

Beyond the platform and the leaning shack that passed for a depot stood a row of wooden buildings. The tallest had a hand-painted sign that said Hotel. Next to it was Lil's Palace. At least she didn't have far to walk to her work. A small separate building with bars on the windows marked Jail stood next to a mouse-gray wooden building with a sign that read Doctor. She thought he must not be very good at his job, because coffins leaned against the outside wall. He could bury his mistakes.

"Ma'am?" A wizened man who might have been eighty—or a worn-out forty—stood with his hat in hand. "Miss Harmonee?"

Hannah stared at him blankly before recovering. "Oh, yes. Mr. Smith?"

"I'll take you to the hotel," he said, replacing his hat.

The parasol offered little relief from the sun, and Hannah squinted at him with half-closed eyes, nodding.

"I'll get someone to bring your baggage over." He motioned to his right.

Hannah turned to where he pointed and was shocked to see two steamer trunks and a locker that looked big enough to be a walk-in closet. Had Mr. Pinkerton secreted a squad of agents in her luggage?

The heat was withering. She could feel sweat beading on her forehead and reached into her handbag to retrieve a handkerchief. What she pulled out made her breath catch in her throat. It was the red bandana she had snatched from the Gentleman Bandit. She had neglected to turn it in with the case file. It still had the faint scent of peppermint.

Hannah hastily shoved it back into her bag. It was imperative that she forget everything but the task at hand. A small voice in her head sent a warning: *Be careful, Hannah.*

13

Cabot Falls, Vermont
Present Day

*J*essop Norton was not all he seemed. Sofia was sure of that. But how could she prove it? She turned into her driveway and shut off the motor. Before she could exit the car, the back door of the house burst open, and Matthew leaped two steps at a time, ending up at the Suburban with one of his well-practiced ninja leaps. "Pow! Zap!" He did a quick bow at the waist. "Mom, you'll never believe what Bryce and me—"

"Bryce and I," Sofia reminded him.

"Okay, you too. We are writing a speech!"

"Good for you," Sofia responded absently. She was glad that Bryce was blending in so well.

Inside, she washed up and mixed the batter for her fruit- and nut-laden muffins. She wanted to send them to the firehouse through Jim as she'd promised the chief. She found baking helpful, and right now, she needed help. There was a question mark tickling the back of her memory, and she couldn't bring it forward. She felt she knew something vital, but she couldn't quite think what.

The aroma of fruit and cinnamon permeated the kitchen. She inhaled deeply, enjoying it and reliving the flood of relief she'd felt when she found Matthew in the tree house. That's when it came to her. When she was looking for Matthew, she had seen a case of charcoal lighter fluid in Norton's garage along with the shell of a vintage sports car he probably intended to restore.

She called Officer Quimby, who promised to pass the information on to the arson investigator. "Of course, there is no law against bulk buying, Mrs. Parker. I'm not sure that qualifies him as a person of interest unless the lab determines that lighter fluid is what started the fire."

Jim came in, stretching. "Are those muffins I smell?"

The oven bell rang. Sofia pulled out four muffin pans and put the remaining two in before she answered. "Yes, two dozen for you to take to the station and the rest to freeze for the celebration. I thought I might take a half dozen over to Mr. Norton."

Jim shook his head. "Sofia, there is no amount of muffins that will warm that man's chilly attitude. Maybe it's time to move on."

"I just can't let it go, Jim," Sofia said as she set the muffins on the cooling racks. "By tomorrow afternoon, we'll have all the repairs done, but he's got all those wrecked machines and so much more damage. I don't know how, but it started on our side."

She started the glaze for the muffins by dribbling vanilla into a butter-and-powdered-sugar mixture. "Uh, do you know anything about what Matthew and Bryce are up to? I was distracted and just happy they were busy."

"Bryce was telling Matthew about his dad's job in the legislature, and somehow that evolved into Matthew wanting to make a speech to the council. He's still smarting about the tree house and lemonade stand. I figured we should let it play out. It'll keep them occupied, and Matthew will learn a little about how government works." Jim laughed. "From the mouths of babes. Who knows what they can accomplish simply because they believe?"

Sofia swirled the tops of the muffins with the icing and placed them in a box. "You can take these to the station when you go."

"And that should be about now. Here's hoping the arsonist

takes a night off. Ned, one of the other volunteers, will help me get the drywall up in the morning. That way, it won't take more than an hour."

"Great. Marla and Julie will help me finish up. I'm anxious to get through the celebration," Sofia admitted.

Bryce and Matthew came in. "We smelled muffins, Aunt Sofia. Are any of them for us?"

"Always," Sofia said. "What are you boys doing in the basement on such a beautiful day?"

"We're going over the laws and regulations for Cabot Falls. I think we found exceptions about separate dwellings that will let us finish the tree house. It looks like the council may have been wrong according to their own rules," Bryce said.

"Zap! Pow!" Matthew said, performing a chopping maneuver in the air. "We got 'em!"

"Also, Uncle Jim, if you and Luke get a post office mailbox for your online business, you should not have any problems selling your birdhouses." Bryce took a muffin in each hand and turned to leave.

A grin crossed Matthew's face. He grabbed two muffins and followed Bryce from the kitchen, leaping and hopping his way out.

Sofia and Jim looked at each other, grinning. "I'm speechless," Sofia admitted. "I just don't know what to say."

When Jim left with the muffins, Sofia thought he'd be gone for the night. She was surprised when he returned a short time later. "Rogers is back from vacation and feeling refreshed enough to take the shift tonight." After a supper of spaghetti and salad, Matthew wanted to practice his speech in front of Sofia and Jim. When he finished, Sofia praised him for such thorough preparation. "But I think I'd rephrase the part calling Norton 'that mean old man.' He's on the council, you know, and you will want to win every vote you can get."

Matthew shrugged. "Yeah, that's what Bryce said."

"Well, he's right, Matthew," Jim said. "But good job. It's open forum at the meeting the day before the Founder's Day celebration. Will you be ready by then?"

Matthew leaped into the air with a kick that narrowly missed the table lamp. "Zap! Pow! Wham!"

"That's enough zaps. Bedtime, everyone," Sofia said, turning out the lamp. She checked the alarm system and followed Jim upstairs to bed.

They had been asleep a few hours when Sofia was awakened by a loud popping noise. The room glowed red. Flashes of flame reflected on the glass in the photos hanging on the opposite wall.

"Jim!" Sofia gasped, shaking him. "Fire!"

A sudden explosion shook the room as the window beside her shattered.

Dry Gulch, Montana
Summer 1871

Hannah's confidence shattered as she stepped off the train platform. A tall, lanky man with a star on his shirt the size of a saucer touched his fingers to his hat. "Ma'am. We sure are looking forward to your show." She was glad to see that the sheriff was carrying the saddlebags containing the replacement payroll.

She returned his greeting with a weak smile. Show? She couldn't carry a tune with a bucket in each hand. She was relieved to see that except for a few horses tethered to posts, the street was abandoned. *At least I won't have many people to disappoint.*

Her hotel room had an iron bed much like the one she had occupied at the orphanage, a side table with an oil lamp, and a dressing table and mirror. The window overlooked the bleak street. When Hannah slid the steamer open, colorful silks, satins, and ostrich feathers spilled into the room. She nearly burst out laughing at the array of exquisite apparel. Perhaps the audience would be so awed by her wardrobe that they wouldn't notice she couldn't sing a lick.

Hannah doubted that, but she thought she'd take the opportunity to see where she was supposed to perform—unless she could come up with a convincing case of laryngitis. Lil's was a large, open room with about two dozen round tables. An elevated stage and a piano were at the back. One of the posters announcing her performance leaned on an easel. Hannah choked back a giggle. Perhaps her most important tool on this assignment was her sense of humor.

"Miss Harmonee? Can I get you something?"

Hannah turned to see a man no taller than five feet four with a mere wreath of dark hair and a mustache that would have put Carlton Vanhiller's to shame. He slung a dish towel over his shoulder and thrust out his hand. "I'm Lil." When Hannah raised an eyebrow, he said, "Short for Little Joe. My dad was Big Joe."

A smile played across her lips. "The hotel clerk said you served meals."

Nodding, he said, "Today's special is buffalo stew. It's on the house for you, Miss Harmonee. Pick any table. I'll find you."

The place was nearly empty. Four men, their faces shadowed beneath their hats, were playing cards. Hannah chose a table near the door. Had Mr. Pinkerton known what he was sending her into? How was she to go about recovering the stolen payroll? Her ridiculous cover was incentive enough to urge her to do so quickly.

Lil set a bowl of buffalo stew and a glass of water on the table, and Hannah nodded in acknowledgment. She kept her eyes on the men. Their heads bobbed as they spoke in low murmurs, occasionally erupting into loud guffaws and snorts. One of them glanced up at her a few times. Had he recognized her? Was he someone she'd met from a previous case, perhaps? Suddenly she realized that he was the soldier who had been assigned to guard the payroll on the train. She recognized him from a photo Mr. Pinkerton had shared with her. She hoped the man didn't know her true identity.

She finished her stew and returned to the hotel, exhausted. Her body still seemed to vibrate from the long, arduous train ride. She could barely keep her eyes open and decided to take a nap. Her eyes closed and she drifted off quickly, but her dreams were filled with the face of the Gentleman Bandit.

A knock on her door startled her awake. *How long have I been asleep?* The room was nearly dark.

"The crowd's gathering at Lil's, Miss Harmonee. They get rowdy pretty quick. You about ready?"

"Soon," she called back. *What was Mr. Pinkerton thinking? A singer?* She removed a taffeta costume the color of the sky from her trunk. It had yards of skirt gathered at the waist and pulled into a bustle the size of a watermelon. She first slipped the double layer of boned crinoline petticoats and then the costume over her head and let the folds fall over. Between the weight and the bulk of the garments, her movements were severely limited.

Selecting a feathered boa to match and a hat covered in blue-dyed feathers, she checked herself in the mirror. She was no Chameleon, but this wasn't bad.

Hannah looped her purse over her wrist. After the incident with the Gentleman Bandit, she rarely left her weapon out of reach. Besides, she thought dryly, she just might need to defend herself once they heard her sing.

Downstairs, Hannah was startled to see that the dark street was jammed with wagons and horses hitched to posts. She entered Lil's and saw that nearly every table was occupied. Besides the men, about half as many women and at least a dozen children of varying ages completed the noisy crowd.

At the back, a man with rolled-up sleeves was playing the piano, although she could barely hear the tinny sound over the noise of the people.

She knew a few songs she could sing while staying on key fairly well, and she gave the list to the pianist: *Goober Peas, Yankee Doodle*, and *Home Sweet Home.*

She walked among the tables as she sang, nodding and smiling as she imagined a real entertainer would do. She paused by the table with the four gamblers from lunchtime. They were so intent on their game that none of them seemed aware that the music had stopped or that she was standing there.

Her eyes focused on the pile of bills in the center of the table. One of the bills bore a mark placed by the U.S. Treasury to identify its money. Careful not to change her expression, she looked at each of the men. Which of them had contributed the marked bill? Her gaze lingered on one of them. Neither the dark hat nor the thick black sideburns were enough of a disguise to distract her from his strong profile. She felt a flood of relief that he was not dead as rumored. Perhaps it was the delicious thought that she could now have the pleasure of arresting him herself. She pulled the red bandana from her purse. "I believe this is yours," she said.

He pushed the hat back on his head and looked up at her, grinning. As casually as if he weren't on the verge of arrest, he tied the bandana around his neck, never taking his focus off her. His eyes danced with mirth beneath the dark, heavy brows. "That color brings out the blue in your eyes. It suits you."

Hannah swallowed the fury at his arrogance as he shoved his chair back and stood. How could she ever have been concerned about his welfare? She wrapped her fingers around the weapon she kept inside her purse.

"Ma'am, may I escort you to the exit? You seem a mite flushed." His pronounced drawl obviously was not natural to him. In her ear, he added, "You might want to keep your Miss Harmonee persona for another day."

Hannah clenched her teeth in a forced smile. She hated that he was right. "Just walk in front of me. And don't try to run. My hand is on my weapon, and my weapon is on you."

He laughed. "I wouldn't dream of it. It seems hardly fair, though, since I had to check mine at the door."

Once outside, with her free hand, Hannah pulled out her handcuffs. "You must've recognized me this afternoon. Why didn't you run?" She almost wished he had.

He shrugged his broad shoulders. "I still had business here in Dry Gulch. Besides, I didn't want to miss the singing debut of Miss Harmonee Rich."

Hannah scoffed. "Stealing on the train wasn't enough for you? You had to go and steal from the government. That puts you in a whole new category, Mr. . . . Mr. . . . ?"

He held his hands out as she raised the handcuffs, and she snapped one cuff on his wrist and the other to the hitching post ring. "Zane," he said. "Just call me Zane." With his free hand, he tipped his hat. "Ma'am." He leaned toward her, and she jerked her head to the left so that his lips merely brushed her cheek.

She felt her cheeks warm. "Try that again, and I'll shoot you, Mr. Zane." He was the one in trouble. Why was she the one so ill at ease? "That should hold you while I locate the sheriff," she told him.

Hannah's shoes thundered on the wood sidewalk as she hurried to the jail as quickly as her costume would allow. Flashing her badge to the surprised lawman, she instructed him to retrieve her captive and hold him until she could escort him back for trial. Meanwhile, surely she could convince him that it was in his best interests to reveal the hiding place of the payroll.

The sheriff holstered his pistol and hurried to keep up with Hannah as she half ran, half loped to the hitching post outside Lil's.

Hannah stopped short, staring in disbelief. One loop of the handcuffs was still attached to the hitching ring. The other hung open and empty.

Zane—if that was really his name—had bested her again. Hannah exploded with fury. If it was the last thing she ever did as a Pinkerton, it would be to have Zane in her custody. It very well might be the last thing she did. An involuntary shudder crept up her spine. Now she had to go inside and face the music.

14

Cabot Falls, Vermont
Present Day

It was several moments before Sofia realized that it was not their home that was on fire—not yet. It was Norton's garage, which was in close proximity to them and could spread.

"Dial 911," Jim instructed as he leaped from bed. "And get the kids out of the house." He spoke calmly, but his voice wavered with anxiety. "I'll get my gear and see what I can do until they get here."

By the time Sofia, the five kids, and Fergus were downstairs and standing across the street, the sirens were close. The fire had already leaped to Norton's house.

"There's someone upstairs!" Vanessa shouted. "Dad, look!"

Jim put his shoulder to the front door, which gave way. He disappeared into the billowing smoke.

"No, Jim," Sofia whimpered as the hose truck hissed to a stop. Volunteers leaped from the truck, unrolled the hose, and hooked it to the hydrant.

"Jim's in there!" Sofia screamed. "He's gone after someone. Do something!"

Just as Chief Benson instructed two men to go in, two figures emerged through the door. Jim pulled Norton, who leaned heavily on him, coughing and wheezing. The EMT rushed forward and helped Jim lay him on the grass and put an oxygen mask to Norton's face.

Pat Cooper, followed by Homer and their poodle, took Sofia's arm. "It's a lot different seeing him in action than just hearing about it, isn't it?"

Sofia realized she was shaking. "It was terrifying to see him run into a burning building. I couldn't even think about Norton being in there. Am I so terrible?"

"What's he doing in there, anyway?" Pat asked. "He's supposed to be staying at the Cabot Falls Inn, isn't he? They're still renovating the house."

Officer Quimby pulled into the cul-de-sac. "Ladies. Mr. Cooper." The young officer continued past them toward the lawn where Norton lay. The volunteers had successfully tamped down the fire, but it had left the garage in ruins and severely damaged the home's outer wall.

Jim spoke briefly with the officer before trotting over to reassure his family that he was no worse for his action. "Norton just kept saying over and over, 'They tried to kill me. They want me dead.' I kept asking him who, but he seems to be in shock."

When the paramedic had checked out Norton and determined that he hadn't inhaled enough smoke to do damage, Quimby took him to the police station to fill out paperwork. Back in their own home, Jim taped a sheet of plastic over the window that had broken from the heat, and Sofia swept the shattered glass into a dustpan and discarded it.

The kids all returned to bed. Jim showered and slid in next to Sofia. "I don't know whether to be proud of you or mad at you," Sofia said. "You scared me so badly, going in there like that."

He wrapped his arm around her. "Truthfully, I'll be more than happy to go back to teaching math in the fall. This has been the toughest thing I've ever done. But I'm glad I did it. I've learned to respect fire and the men and women who fight it, but I'm careful. I had to go in after Norton, or it could have been a real tragedy."

"I know," she conceded. "I agree."

Jim grinned. "Besides, now maybe the chief will let me run the siren!"

Sofia laughed and playfully poked him on the shoulder. "Go to sleep! This doesn't get you out of hanging drywall tomorrow!"

The next morning, they learned that a second fire had broken out that night while Norton was at the police station, but Sofia still was not ready to remove him from her list of suspects. "What if he has a partner?" she asked Marla as they painted the newly installed wall.

"It is entirely possible that he is both unlikable and innocent, but I think it's time to move on," Marla said. "That's about what I've had to do, locating proof that Herbert Cabot founded Cabot Falls and incorporated it, including all the surrounding land where he built the inn. I'm about out of options. But I had a little luck on your research, Sofia. I'm surprised you haven't asked lately."

Sofia laid her brush across the paint can and rubbed her temples. "I have had so much on my mind, I guess I just shoved it aside. What did you find out?"

"When I didn't have any luck with the Chicago archives, I asked a librarian friend of mine to check in with the Smithsonian, and since she is a professional researcher, they let her go through the stuff from the Pinkerton Agency that they are still categorizing. There were copies of telegraph communications that indicated Hannah Reed went out West, apparently on assignment. She apparently had a number of aliases."

"You mean, like in hiding?" Sofia asked.

"No, like in disguises. Apparently she worked undercover a lot of the time," Marla said. "Her reports were too long to copy and email. My friend is sending them priority. It should make interesting reading."

Sofia shrugged. "That's interesting, but I still don't know how Hannah Reed is related to me or what she has to do with the initials A.J. and those weird letters along the edge. Until I can find a connection to her, I have to assume that she was perhaps a friend of relatives, as much as I'd like to have such a bold woman in the family tree." Sofia's cell phone rang. It was her sister Gina, once again checking on Bryce. "He was in no danger, nor was anyone else, Gina. I keep my family safe from harm, and Bryce is part of my family too."

"I'm not saying you can't, little sister. My trouble is that I miss him. We're thinking of coming for the celebration, and then he can come back with us," Gina said.

"He and Matthew will be so disappointed. They're working on a presentation to the city council here. Why don't you come early? The boys can move to the tent, and you can have their room."

"Uh, we'll just stay at the inn," Gina said.

"It's Founder's Day weekend, Gina. The inn and everything else is sold out."

"Oh, nonsense. Inns always save a room for celebrities and dignitaries."

Sofia said goodbye and hung up. She repeated Gina's conversation. Marla laughed. "Well, the inn does have a presidential suite that remains all dressed up just in case they get a special visitor. I suspect a senator from Massachusetts is about as close as they'll ever get to a presidential visit," Marla said.

"Meanwhile, I am going next door to see if I can help Mr. Norton clean up," Sofia said.

She hoped her friends would go with her, but if not, she'd go alone.

Dry Gulch, Montana
Summer 1871

Alone in her hotel room, Hannah was still angry. Standing before the mirror, she chastised herself for being so gullible. *That . . . that Zane!* He was slipperier than a snake and just as low. *He—* She stopped her silent rant and stared at her image. Was blue really her best color? He'd said that it brought out the color of her eyes. "Hannah, what's wrong with you?" she said aloud. "You are losing your grip on the important things, like catching that thief."

She shrugged out of the elaborate taffeta dress and rehung it in the steamer. She wasn't Harmonee Rich. She was Hannah Reed, Pinkerton operative, and she felt like an idiot. Zane had eluded her once again.

She changed into her cotton nightgown and turned down the kerosene lamp until its flame flickered and disappeared, plunging the room into darkness. She raised the shade, pausing to look at the Milky Way slashing through the sky like a rip in dark velvet cloth.

She lay on the bed, gathering her thoughts. Zane had graduated from passenger theft to robbing the military. Well, technically, the money belonged to the U.S. Treasury, and the rail company was liable for it.

"And how do you know which of the cardplayers had the

marked bill?" Kate would have asked her. "And do you know how he got it? You must have proof."

Did she really know that Zane was the thief? The marked bill was on the table with a pile of money. There were three others at the table. Like an amateur, she hadn't even considered them. That was only one bill. She needed to find the whole payroll to reveal the thief. Or she needed to prove who the thief was in order to find the payroll. She knew one thing for sure: She must not fail.

Even if Zane was not the payroll thief, he was a train robber. How had he escaped the shootout against the Secret Service and a posse of Pinkertons? She rolled to her side, smiling against her will. Why wouldn't he escape them? He had escaped her twice. He was as slippery as a greased pig. Despite her frustration, she found him fascinating. His smile was both irritating and attractive; his teeth were star-white against his olive complexion. And she hadn't been wrong about his nose; it was definitely Romanesque.

Suddenly, an object sailed through the open window and landed with a thud on the floor near the bed. Hannah grabbed her weapon, rolled toward the window, and hastened to her feet in time to see the silhouette of a man on a horse disappear behind the mercantile. She quickly relit the oil lamp and retrieved the thrown object, a rock with a note wrapped inside a red bandana permeated with a faint aroma of peppermint.

What you're looking for is in Room 208.

She dropped to a sitting position on the side of the bed. *What*, it said, not *who*. The note had to be from Zane. Could he be telling her where the payroll money was? If he thought she'd give up just because . . . *Ooh, what an exasperating man.* At least he was still in town; there was a chance she could find him quickly.

Hannah changed into a white blouse and a dark cotton skirt. She slid into a pair of soft slippers and thrust the pistol into her skirt pocket. Stepping into the empty hallway, she crept to room 208 and rapped softly on the door. When there was no answer, she pulled a pin from her hair and jiggled it in the lock until it opened. It was so quiet that all she could hear was her own breathing.

Hannah silently slid the drawers open, rifling through their contents. *Nothing suspicious there.* She knelt down to peer under the bed. There lay the leather saddlebag marked U.S. Treasury. She was just about to grab it when she heard the shuffle of feet outside the door. She quickly slid under the bed just as the door opened.

She watched breathlessly as cavalry boots approached the bed. She pressed her cheek to the floor as the springs above her sagged beneath the man's weight. A hand reached under the bed, pulling at the saddlebag. Moments later, grunting, he shoved it back, nearly crushing her nose. The springs creaked as he stood. Hannah glimpsed him in the mirror's reflection. It was the soldier guard she had recognized from the card game.

Hannah waited until he left and then scooted from under the bed. With the saddlebag draped over her shoulder, she followed him to Lil's. Once the cavalryman was seated, Hannah strode up to the table, her weapon drawn, and dropped the bag on the table. "You're in a great deal of trouble, soldier," she said, quickly handcuffing the culprit.

The men in Lil's were agape, watching Miss Harmonee commandeer the young man. She produced her badge, assuring the crowd that she had the situation perfectly in hand.

"Sure glad to hear you're a better lawman than a singer," someone yelled from the back of the saloon.

"The next wisecrack like that will get you in shackles too." Hannah turned to one of the other men. "Fetch the sheriff." No more letting a suspect out of her sight.

When the payroll and the soldier—Corporal Anson Trapp— were safely locked away, Hannah returned to her room to get as much sleep as she could. Tomorrow she'd escort the replacement payroll to the fort and then catch the first eastbound train out of Dry Gulch. She'd leave it to Mr. Pinkerton to hash out who would get the prisoner and whether it was a federal crime or a military offense punishable by court-martial.

Hannah snuggled under the bedsheet, smiling, though she wasn't quite sure why. Yes, she was happy to have put her case to rest. But as it turned out, it wasn't Zane. She had mixed feelings about that. He must have recognized that the money Trapp used was marked. He was certainly clever enough to put the clues together. And he had told her where to find the money.

Did he hope that she'd forget about him as the Gentleman Bandit? He had momentarily endeared himself by returning her locket. Had he been as reluctant a robber as she had been a pickpocket? No, he enjoyed it, and he enjoyed taunting her.

She finally fell asleep. When she awoke in the morning, she felt flushed from her dreams. He had haunted her even there. Would she ever see him again? If so, she'd have to arrest him.

Hannah checked with the sheriff to be sure the prisoner and the money were safe. Then she telegraphed the office with news of her progress but decided to wait until she saw Mr. Pinkerton in person before revealing that Zane was alive. The colonel at the fort was sending armed escorts to get the payroll. She had the feeling Mr. Pinkerton would want her to see the payroll to the fort, just as a precaution.

Hannah looked up as the telegraph machine came to life, clattering its code that only the trained clerk could understand.

When he handed her the scribbled note, she moaned. It seemed that she was not through with this gritty landscape yet.

CIVILIAN MURDER FORT GRIMM STOP
FIND KILLER STOP

Her heart sank. Find the killer? Just like that? But if she was ever going to make it home in time for Christmas, she knew she'd better figure it out. All she had to do was learn about the victim, figure out who would want him or her dead, and why. Oh, and prove it all—or get a confession.

Hannah looked up as two army supply wagons and an escort of six men on horseback ambled into town, kicking up dust from the street.

A long, haunting whistle sounded in the distance. "Train's coming," the sheriff said. "The colonel's missus and their children are on board. They're joining him from back East."

Hannah hoped their arrival wouldn't complicate the investigation. "Stall them from leaving without me, Sheriff. I'll be staying there for a few days." She rushed back to her room and hastily threw a few of the plainer dresses into a carpet bag she ordinarily used for her supplies and then hurried back to the area in front of the jail.

An exhausted-looking woman was trying unsuccessfully to corral four children who looked to range in age from four to nine. Just as she snagged one, another broke away. Hannah smiled. *Like herding cats,* she thought. The woman was definitely going to need the cavalry to help round them up. Several men in army uniforms loaded baskets, luggage, and several plush leather chairs onto one of the wagons.

Hannah snatched a little boy by his suspenders just in time to keep him from tumbling headfirst into a water trough. She carried the wiggling little fellow and set him down in front of his mother.

While waiting for the entourage to depart for the fort, one of the soldiers told her that the victim was a civilian woman who had lived on the post and worked as a housekeeper for Colonel Ezra Liam Malone, who had been at the post only six months.

The timing of his wife's arrival couldn't have been worse. Or perhaps the murder was because of the wife's arrival. What if the colonel considered the woman more than a servant? What if she hadn't wanted to give up her position to the wife?

Hannah hoped she would prove him innocent. She wanted to believe that most husbands loved their wives and that most mothers loved their children. She wanted her life and those at the orphanage to be anomalies. The soldiers brought out the saddlebag with the payroll and tucked it between several pieces of luggage.

Hannah climbed aboard the wagon carrying the bulk of the furniture. Mrs. Malone and her rambunctious offspring boarded the other.

Hannah hoped this wouldn't take long. If she could pick up the trail of the elusive Zane . . . An uninvited smile played across her lips. A gentleman robber who returns jewelry, a gambler who points to a robber—who was he, really? She had to know more, no matter what it cost her.

15

Cabot Falls, Vermont
Present Day

"So it costs me my pride; it's a small price to pay," Sofia told Marla and Julie. "I know Jessop Norton is a pain, but maybe he has a reason." She sighed wearily and picked up the sponge and bucket. "Well, I'm going, and that's that."

Julie shrugged. "Hold on. I'm coming too."

"Me too," Marla said, "but I'm doing this for you, Sofia."

Norton looked up, frowning, as the trio entered.

"We're here to help," Sofia said. "We can start scrubbing away soot."

"Why?" he asked.

"Why does everyone keep asking me that? Because that's what neighbors do, Mr. Norton," Sofia replied. She filled the bucket with water.

"But—but . . ." he stammered, obviously flustered.

Sofia smiled. "You sound like a bad lawn mower. Are you going to just watch us, or are you going to work? I see you have a new window."

"You need drapes," Marla said. "Nobody wants passersby seeing them exercise. I go to Grand Point. It'll be nice to have a gym close to work."

Julie laughed. "It's the end of my excuses not to exercise."

"Ladies, please!" Norton spoke loudly, and there was a distinct edge in his voice. "Leave! I don't want your help, don't you understand? Go on, get out!"

Shocked, Sofia grabbed the bucket. "We're going, Mr. Norton. But just remember that we tried to help. I don't know what your problem is, but leave me and my family out of it from now on."

Back in her shop, she dumped the water into the sink. When the others had done the same, she wiped the sink dry. "How can anybody be so cantankerous?"

Julie touched her arm sympathetically. "You did your best. Just forget him."

Marla crossed her arms and waggled her head so that her blond waves bounced. "If you were as familiar with a gym as I am, you wouldn't be so surprised. He's hiding something, and I know what."

Sofia stared at her. "Well, are you going to share?"

"I suspected something was wrong when I saw the step machine. Did you see how twisted the handles were? The fire couldn't have gotten that intense without burning the shop to the ground. I looked at the model number on the plate. It was not a new machine. All of those machines were useless before the fire."

Sofia leaned back against the counter. "But he was yelling that night about how he'd just gotten them all out of the boxes and installed."

Julie said, "I noticed that he hadn't installed extra wiring or a bigger breaker box. I read about businesses burned for insurance after substituting old furniture and equipment; it takes a lot of planning and cooperation."

Sofia snapped her fingers. "Jim said Norton kept saying 'They tried to kill me' as the paramedic was giving him oxygen."

"Who?" Marla asked.

"I don't know," Sofia replied. "He denied that he'd said it, although both Jim and the EMT heard him. He told Officer

Quimby he'd just been in shock. If he won't talk, there's nothing any of us can do." She sighed wearily. "Thanks for your help today."

Back home, Sofia couldn't stop thinking about what Marla had said. When she'd showered, she put on a pot of tea and invited her neighbor over for some. She told Pat about the machines over crumb cake and peach tea.

"It sounds like insurance fraud to me," Pat said. "Or maybe the mob." Pat was an avid fan of television crime shows. "Norton is certainly a 10-66."

"What's that?" Sofia asked Pat.

"That's ten-code for suspicious person. He couldn't pull this off alone. An insurance adjuster would know they were props. If he wrote Norton a check, then he's either not very good at his job or he's part of the fraud." Pat put her cup down and dabbed her mouth with the napkin. "Don't go trying to solve this on your own, Sofia. It could be dangerous."

When Pat left, Sofia called Officer Quimby and told him what she knew.

"Yes ma'am. Inspector O'Leary recognized it right away. Just don't say anything to anybody. We have several persons of interest."

Satisfied that she'd done all she could do, Sofia jotted down a list of pies she might offer the inn since there would be more demand during the Founder's Day celebration. She then drove to the inn to discuss her plans with the manager.

Pulling into the parking lot, she saw Norton in a loud discussion with two men. One she recognized as the insurance agent. The other she didn't know, but she guessed he might be the third corner of the triangle. Sofia made note of his slight build, sandy blond hair, and lighter, close-cut beard.

When she returned home, she quickly sketched the features of the third man while they were fresh in her memory and then called Gina to tell her about the suite. "Incidentally, did you ever hear Nonna talk about a Pinkerton detective ancestor?"

"I do remember a badge that said *Pinkerton* in her costume jewelry box. I thought it was a prop for a costume one of our uncles might have worn. I gave it to Bryce to play with. You mean it could be real?"

"I think so, Gina. I just don't know how the woman fits into the family. I can't find any other Reeds. I'm beginning to wonder if we have a skeleton in the family closet."

"I have every confidence in your ability to sort it through, Sofia. See you soon."

Sofia smiled as she disconnected the call. *Every confidence, huh?* she thought. *Well, that's one of us.* She'd felt she would have personally had a lot more confidence if she knew more about Norton.

Fort Grimm, Montana
Autumn 1871

What at first had seemed a mirage in the heat waves rising out of the parched earth materialized into Fort Grimm—a dull, faded, high wall with square towers on both sides of the tall gates. The only color was the flag, which hung limply against the pole, as there was no hint of a breeze.

Hannah's parasol offered no defense against the sun. Overhead, a large bird screeched like an unoiled door hinge and spiraled downward on a thermal, flapping away at the last moment.

"Hawk," the driver said, although she hadn't asked.

Several teepees were clustered outside the fence. "Nakoda," he said. He was a man of few words. The gates opened, and the two wagons entered. A rugged man in a cavalry officer's uniform strode from one of the buildings as the Malone children leaped from the wagon, shrieking, "Daddy, Daddy!"

Laughing, he scooped all four to him before standing to embrace his wife. Hannah smiled, hoping she would do nothing to break up this happy little reunion. The colonel certainly didn't look like an errant husband.

Hannah retrieved the saddlebag with the payroll and, after giving the couple time to reconnect, held it high above her head to get his attention.

He disengaged from the clinging children and motioned to an officer. "The paymaster will take that; the men certainly will be glad too. I'm Colonel Malone, and you must be the Pinkerton agent. I'm glad to get an outside investigator. I don't want any questions later about a cover-up."

He told her that the victim, Amanda di Ponte, was his housekeeper and that he had found her dead on his kitchen floor. The army doctor, who said he thought it was poison, was not really a doctor at all but someone who could remove bullets and arrows and patch the men up if they got in a brawl.

Hannah took down the information as he spoke and then asked to see the body, which they had stored in the stockade.

Hannah removed the sheet. There were no bruises or defensive injuries. Her skin was an odd shade of tan. Hannah frowned. "Was she of Indian heritage?" When the colonel said no, Hannah stood. "You can bury her now. I've seen enough. May I see where you found her?"

"The kitchen in my quarters. Yes, of course," the colonel said.

Hannah removed the barrier across the kitchen door to keep others from contaminating the scene. After seeing the condition of the body, she had a suspicion about the cause of death. Kate had once told her of a similar-looking corpse. *I just need to find—ah, yes. There it is.* She had been right in her guess. On the shelf above the stove, the colonel's tobacco tin lay on its side with the lid off. Its contents were spread along the shelf right to the edge. She was right.

Hannah found the colonel sitting on the edge of his porch, watching his children playing with someone's scraggly little dog. She stepped off the porch and sat next to him. "Your men may leave the fort when you wish, Colonel. There is no murderer among you. The woman died a tragic and avoidable death, but it was purely accidental."

His face seemed to light with relief. "But what happened?"

"You are a lucky man, Colonel. Had you drunk the coffee, your wife would have arrived a widow. Your housekeeper died of direct and gross nicotine poisoning. I suspected as much when I saw her skin. I found a thick residue of tobacco in the bottom of a cup and in the coffeepot, where it spilled from a shelf above. There are cases of tobacco farmers dying from absorbing high doses through their skin. Now they wear gloves while handling the leaves. It can be quite lethal in large, pure doses. Ingested in the coffee, it was even more lethal and swift."

She arose. "Now I'd like to be on my way." Hannah felt really good. It was satisfying to discover that there was no murder and no murderer.

Zane was probably long gone. Still, she had the feeling that he was not totally out of her life. Oddly, the thought didn't disturb her as much as it should have.

Back in Dry Gulch, Hannah telegraphed headquarters.

*CASE SOLVED STOP ACCIDENTAL DEATH STOP
COMING HOME STOP*

Hannah had expected a "good job" or "hurry home" message. Instead, she had an almost immediate response.

NOT YET STOP

"Home" was no more than a sparsely furnished room and a mysterious baby quilt, but Hannah was beginning to wonder if she'd ever see it again, or if she had become the unofficial western branch of the Pinkerton Detective Agency. She sank into a chair to read the remainder of the note.

The telegraph instructed Hannah to remain in Dry Gulch and wait for a Miss Penelope Partridge to arrive and fill her in on a missing person and a possible grand theft.

She had lunch at Lil's—buffalo stew again—and returned to her room at the hotel, where she stayed until there was a rap on her door.

"A Miss Partridge is in the lobby to see you," the clerk said through the door. "Do you want her to come up or—"

"No, I'll come down. Thank you," she said, stowing the book she was reading in the steamer trunk pocket.

Penelope Partridge was every inch the perfect image of a schoolmarm, with her hair severely pulled back and pinned in a tight bun at the nape of her neck, a plain gray dress, and no jewelry. Yet she seemed to be barely holding herself together, and the moment Hannah introduced herself, Miss Partridge melted into a pool of tears.

Hannah placed a consoling hand on her shoulder. When the woman was again in control of herself, she said, "So, Miss Partridge, Mr. Pinkerton said that he and your father are good friends back East. He heard that Mr. Partridge had come out West to speculate in mining. Tell me why you are concerned."

"Please, call me Penny. I received this letter three months ago. I haven't heard from him since. I'm sure something is wrong."

Hannah read the letter. In it, her father said he believed he was close to filing a claim to a silver mine. He had discovered a vein but wanted to be sure it was a major find before filing. *Just a couple more dynamite blasts, and I'll let you know.*

"He isn't an experienced prospector," Penny said. "He has a mining degree, but I worried about him being out here alone. I urged him to get a knowledgeable partner. If he is injured out there by himself, he'd have no one to help him or to go for help. I am so afraid that he has perished." Penny dabbed at her red-rimmed eyes. "He's all I have, Detective. My mother died when I was a child. He raised me alone. He did office work for a mining company while I was growing up so that I wouldn't be raised by strangers. Exploration was his first love, but he gave that up for me."

Hannah felt heavyhearted. "You are his first love, Penny. He proved that." She fought back tears of her own. *A parent who really loves his child.* She had never known that. She desperately wanted to find this woman's father for her. "I see the last sentence is not complete. Are there other pages?"

"Oh yes. Father was something of an artist in his spare time— just a hobby, you understand. But he always put a little sketch at the end of his letters, a little gift for me."

"Do you have all of his letters?"

Penny dug into her handbag and retrieved a stack of folded papers tied together with a pink ribbon. Hannah shifted in her chair, as it reminded her of her mysterious quilt back home. "Please take care of these, won't you?"

Hannah nodded. "There may be something he wrote or

something he sketched that will help—something that you didn't see, but I will. Are you staying at this hotel?" Penny assured her that she would wait there no matter how long it took. Hannah learned from the sheriff that the assayer's office was down the rails a whistle-stop away in a settlement called Greentown. She arranged to board the westbound train.

Hannah realized she had only the remotest chance of finding a mine somewhere in the miles upon miles of uninhabited landscape. If she did figure it out, she hoped for Penny's sake that she'd find her father harvesting silver and that he'd simply lost count of the days. She was afraid she would find a crime scene instead. Silver, gold, gems—too many people had the wrong values. The woman just wanted her father.

Hannah had an odd feeling about this. All those years in the orphanage, and now on her own, she had been haunted by the thought that her mother had abandoned her. What about her father? What if not one but two people hadn't wanted her? She was beginning to dread what she might find.

She knew only that it was something she had to do.

16

Cabot Falls, Vermont
Present Day

*S*ofia was running out of space at home, so she took boxes of cakes and muffins to the shop freezer and fridge. Finished, she dialed her father. Lou Nelson lived about an hour away from Cabot Falls.

"Dad, do you ever remember anyone in the family mentioning a woman detective, a Pinkerton? Or do you remember a Hannah Reed or having an Irish ancestor?"

"I do vaguely remember your great-grandmother talking about an ancestor who was ahead of her time. She got tighter than a clam when your mother wanted to know more. She said something like, 'We don't talk about that.' I don't think it was ever mentioned again, and I hadn't thought about it until now."

"If you can find anything that has a 'Hannah' or anything about anyone with the initials A.J., would you bring it with you when you come for the Founder's Day celebration?"

"I seem to remember a Hannah or two, or maybe Anna. I hadn't thought about that. Let me take a look in the attic. I think there are a couple of family Bibles and some documents in an old trunk."

"Thanks, Dad. Love you." Sofia hung up. She decided to bake one more big batch of muffins. She wanted to do what she called goodwill snooping. She filled a basket while the muffins were still warm and covered them with a red-checked napkin. Starting at

Letitia Leake's Party Specialties next door to La Dolce Vita, Sofia passed out complimentary muffins. She learned that Letitia and Gregg Barker, who owned Post Cards, Etc., had a running feud because Letitia carried invitations, which he considered his purview. She discovered that Everett Joye, owner of the Joye-Full Noise musical instruments store, had tried to form a barbershop quartet for Founder's Day but was rebuffed by Wilson Watson, the banker. "Always slapping people on the back while he turns them down for a loan," Everett said. "Besides, who doesn't like to sing barbershop?"

Before she handed out the last muffin, she had heard all the gossip beneath the surface of the quaint shops around which the intrigue swirled. She learned that Mark Keeler, the real estate agent who was in charge of the leases for the shops as well as many of the destroyed buildings, was slow to make repairs. Although he had struck Sofia as friendly and always willing to help people land a good deal, even if he had to sacrifice part of his commission, she realized that maybe his friendliness ended when the contract was signed. Celia Kraft, who owned Kraft's Crafts, said that her wiring needed to be replaced because many of the receptacles no longer worked. She said Keeler finally had the repairs made only when she threatened to go to the mayor.

Robert Bradford, owner of The Book Shelf, said Keeler balked at paying for a broken water pipe that flooded his place, ruining books on the lower shelves and warping the bookcases. "He even suggested that I could break the lease."

Keeler's real estate office was at the far end of the shops. By the time Sofia entered it, she had a different portrait of Keeler. She was surprised to see he was wearing a cast on his arm. "I fell," he told her. "Fell off a ladder changing a lightbulb."

Sofia frowned. He had told one owner that he'd had a boating accident and another that a bookshelf fell on his arm. *What's going on with this guy?* Had he been doing something illegal when he broke his arm? *It's never hard to remember the truth. But it isn't uncommon for people who are lying to forget what they said previously.* She prided herself on her sense of smell, her ability to detect and identify aromas, which was essential for a good chef. Right now, she was detecting the distinct odor of a burn gel.

Sofia took her empty basket and hurried to the other end of the strip, where her Suburban was parked. She slid behind the wheel but didn't start the car. Instead, she mulled over what she had learned. Keeler handled the property for the Cabot Foundation as well as other properties near downtown. He was hesitant to make repairs, which was definitely the responsibility of the owners and not the renters. It was certainly necessary to keep up the repairs or lose the renters. But why would he want to lose the renters?

"Unless he had other plans for the shops. But what?" she asked aloud. He seemed to be huddling with Norton a lot. She'd thought it normal, considering the burned-out shop, but what if something else had drawn them together?

Her phone rang. The caller ID showed it was her dad. "I found a child's Bible in one of the boxes, Sofia. In the front it says, 'This Bible is the property of Miss Hannah Reed, Whiteside Orphanage, Chicago, Illinois.' Does that help?"

"It tells me that Hannah Reed probably is an ancestor and we just haven't found the connection. Why else would the Bible be in our possession? I can't imagine that Mom had it without a reason. But I wonder if we know her parents. At least we know that we have a pretty daring woman in our ranks. Dad, there are women in law enforcement everywhere now who owe their thanks to women like Hannah Reed. She wasn't the first female Pinkerton agent. Kate Warne was. But it was still uncommon in Hannah's day." Sofia felt a sense of pride and a renewed determination. "But if we can't find her parents and we can't find her descendants, how do we know that she really is family?"

Mr. Nelson paused for a moment. "I'll keep looking. But remember this, Sofia. Nonna took great pride in family and in that quilt, or she wouldn't have left it to you. She knew that you'd figure it out. I'd better get back to the attic. You've whetted my curiosity about this woman now."

Sofia turned the key and the Suburban rumbled to life. She backed out and headed home. She'd learned a lot about the past and the present today, and she needed to work all of it out in her thoughts. If she had her choice, she would remain with the past, where it was safely over, no matter what she discovered.

The present wasn't so easy to deal with. Were the fires all some sort of master plan perpetrated by these businessmen? What did anyone really know about Norton or Keeler? Could someone else be in on it, someone they wouldn't suspect? There was no way she could sit back and wait for the authorities to plod through this. She wouldn't be true to Hannah Reed if she walked away just as she discovered a major clue.

Greentown, Montana
Autumn 1871

All Hannah knew about Greentown was what the sheriff of Dry Gulch had warned her about—that it wasn't nearly as nice as his town. "If I was you, I wouldn't be flashing that badge around there."

Hannah thought that under the circumstances, he had a good point. She might get more information if she pretended to be a reporter from back East. While she waited for the westbound train to arrive, she perused the letters from Partridge to his daughter.

She smiled at the sweetness of his tone and his obvious concern for her welfare.

He had drawn a little partridge tucked safely under the wing of a larger bird on every letter, like a reminder that he always had her best interests at heart. At the end of each missive, he had drawn a different landscape. Perhaps they were sights he passed. His work would never see an art gallery, but it wasn't bad.

Greentown was even worse than Dry Gulch. It had been named after John Green, its founder, and not for beautiful pastures, as Hannah had imagined. But somewhere in the vicinity was an ore mine, if Mr. Partridge had been correct. If he had found silver amid the other metals, she was sure that the U.S. Treasury would want to contract with him. It needed silver for coins.

Greentown had a small hotel, the Green Hotel. It was right next to the John Green Mercantile, which was next to Green Dry Goods, which was next to John Green Hardware, which was next door to the assay office—John Green, Proprietor.

Mrs. Green, a hefty woman with graying hair and a complexion that mirrored the dry landscape, was at the hotel's registry desk. "My my, we don't get many nicely dressed young ladies, just grubby ol' prospectors." She shoved the registry book toward Hannah.

Hannah wrote slowly so she could read the names of previous guests. Partridge had last been here several months ago. It was not a good sign.

Mrs. Green turned the book around. "Okay . . . Miss Jenkins, is it?"

"Yes, Amanda Jenkins. I'm here to do a human interest story about prospectors and mining."

Mrs. Green pushed a few wayward strands of hair behind her ears. "We haven't ever had a reporter out here before. How exciting. If there's anything you want to know, I'm glad to help. My given name's Rebekah, that's R-E—"

"Thank you, Mrs. Green. Later, perhaps. I just want to put my things in my room."

The woman handed her a key. "First door on the left. That's *Rebekah* with an *H*; not everyone uses an *H*, but I do," she called after Hannah.

Hannah unpacked and put the contents in the dresser drawer. She opened the window although there was not enough of a breeze to ruffle the gauze curtain. She flopped onto the side of the bed, fanning herself with the red bandana. She smiled wistfully, wondering how many more times it would exchange hands between her and Zane.

She shrugged dismissively. If he were wise, he probably had headed back East to lose himself in one of the crowded cities. She'd probably never see him again.

Hannah pinned her Pinkerton badge on the underside of her skirt. She couldn't chance having Mrs. Green or someone else finding it. She was well aware that people sometimes snooped. *Where to start looking for Partridge?* she wondered. A visit to the assayer's office seemed like a good idea; she could see if he had registered the claim before he disappeared.

Mr. Green was as thin as his wife was not. His blue eyes seemed to dance behind a pair of wire-rimmed glasses, which he shoved down and peered over when Hannah entered. "Oh, Miss Jenkins."

Word traveled fast in a town that was only a hundred yards long. They probably knew a great deal about everyone who came here. "I am writing an article—"

"I know—human interest, right?"

Hannah felt as if she had been thrown off her focus. "On prospecting," she finished. "Of course, I will want to hear all your interesting stories, Mr. Green. But before I do that, I want to speak with some of the men who have registered claims, and I'd like to see a mine for myself. I want to follow the process chronologically."

"Chronological, you say? That means in order, right? Then you have to start at the John Green Hardware next door. It wouldn't do them any good to go looking without the tools of their trade, now would it?"

What Hannah really wanted to see was the assayer's claims list, but she needed his full cooperation. "Yes, of course. I know where it is. I'll go there first." Hannah sashayed out of the assay office, down the boardwalk and up the steps to the hardware store. Upon entering, she was startled to find Mr. Green behind the counter, slightly out of breath.

"Back door and fast walking," he said. "May I help you with your story, Miss Jenkins?"

Hannah tried to smother a laugh that erupted in an unladylike snort. "Yes, you may, Mr. Green. Please show me everything a miner would purchase here."

"There's the hat with the metal plate to hold the candle, and the candle spike so they can work without having to hold a light, the ore bucket, and the lunch bucket. And the picks, of course."

"Do you keep a list of customers?" Hannah asked. She hoped to learn the last time Partridge had purchased anything.

"Only the ones with running accounts. They pay at the end of the month. But tool purchases are usually only one time. Green Dry Goods sells lots of britches. Stuffing ore in the pockets of their britches causes lots o' rips and tears. My missus repairs 'em a few times, but there's a limit to what material can take. At the Green Mercantile, I sell a good bit of jerky and beans to them. And tea or coffee, of course. There's nothing confidential about the lists, but they're separated by stores, if you want to look through them. I hear that reporters are pretty snoopy."

Returning to the assayer's office, Hannah finally got to examine the claims list, but discovered that Partridge had never registered a mining claim. Mr. Green had met Patridge at the hardware store, but not in his capacity of assayer. Whatever happened to Patridge had occurred after his letter to his daughter. Hannah noticed there was a claim filed by a Josiah Talltree only a week after the date on Partridge's last letter. "Is this man a Nakoda?" she asked Mr. Green.

"No ma'am, he's one of those eastern dandies. Dressed way too fancy to be working a claim. But sure enough, he pranced in here a few days after that Partridge fella with a map and directions and staked it out. I would never have believed it if I hadn't seen it. He claimed he had 'the gift,' whatever that means."

Hannah scowled. "I thought I might just take a ride out." She had a hunch that the drawings in Partridge's letters might be more significant than his daughter thought. She wanted to see Talltree's mine for herself.

"Well, if you're dead set on it, you need to forget those fancy eastern clothes and get some britches. We have only western saddles at Green Horse Stables."

Hannah purchased several water canteens and a shotgun from the hardware, britches from the dry goods store, and jerky from the mercantile. *Greentown may get rich on the Pinkertons,* she thought.

She copied the map, rented a horse from the stables, and set out on a well-worn path leading toward the mountains. A multitude of smaller paths spiked out from the more heavily traveled trail, but she ignored them. She figured instinct, Kate's training, and Partridge's sketches would let her know when to leave the main trail.

She found vague signs of former campfires, where he or others had lingered. She had been intent on following the sketch clues for some time when she suddenly realized the air was getting chilly. The sun was in descent. Even if she turned back immediately, she knew she wouldn't reach Greentown before sunset. There was still a little daylight, so Hannah thought she might as well keep going as long as she could.

Just ahead, coming toward her, Hannah saw a man on horseback leading a pack mule loaded with miner's tools. As they neared each other, she noted a thick mane of gray hair protruding from under the man's hat; it was tied at the nape of his neck by a rawhide string. His long, tangled, white beard was thick enough to hold a bird's nest. He looked as she'd imagined prospectors looked after months out here. His head was down, and for a moment, Hannah thought he was sleeping. As they met each other, he reined in his horse and spoke in a voice stronger than she'd expected: "You shouldn't be out here alone."

Startled, she said, "Obviously, I'm not alone. You're out here."

"Nightfall comes quick out here. It's best to set up camp before it happens." When he lifted his face, Hannah nearly fell off her horse. No amount of phony gray hair could hide those emerald eyes. *Zane.* She pretended she hadn't recognized him. With a little luck, she could get him back to Greentown before he knew he had been found out.

"I read once about building a lean-to out of sticks and brush. I'll be all right." She bristled at the sound of his muffled laugh.

"I have a tent," he said. Those brilliant white teeth made his beard look murky by comparison.

"Good for you!"

"I mean, you can sleep in the tent," he said as patiently as if he were speaking to a child.

Hannah flushed. "Certainly not!"

"I'll bed down by the campfire. You can sleep in the tent alone, Miss . . .?"

"Jenkins . . . Amanda Jenkins." If he could play this game, so could she. "I will sleep by the campfire," Hannah said, "down the path from you."

"You know how to build a campfire, Miss Amanda Jenkins?" he asked.

Hannah's shoulders drooped in defeat. She had brought jerky, water, and even a shotgun in case of wild animals or worse. But she'd never thought about matches. "I . . . I guess I can accept your hospitality, Mr. . . . .?" Just what alias would she add to Gentleman Bandit and Zane the Gambler?

"Folks call me Porcupine," he said. "I'll give you some matches."

"Porcupine. Very apt," she said, smiling. Hannah slid off her horse. "Stay," she instructed it.

He laughed. "You need to hobble him so he can move around and graze but can't go running back to the barn and leave you high and dry."

Hannah had no idea how to hobble a horse. Besides, it sounded mean. "Maybe I can just tie his reins to my wrist."

Zane dismounted. "Not unless you want to be dragged home by your wrist. Allow me."

In short order, he had the saddles and backpack removed, the animals hobbled, and a campfire going. He set an open can of beans on a stone next to the fire and poured water into a small coffeepot, adding the grounds before he sat on the trunk of a fallen tree next to Hannah.

"What brings you out here, Miss Jenkins? You don't look like a typical prospector."

She smiled. He looked exactly like a typical prospector, thanks to his meticulous disguise. She might have changed her name, but she still had the mahogany-red hair and the row of freckles across her nose. Her miner's khaki britches did not fool him. Well, the joke was on him. She wasn't fooled either. She saw right through all that gray hair and beard—right through to those wickedly teasing green eyes.

"I'm writing articles on ore mining for my newspaper." She

added, "I'm looking for a prospector by the name of Partridge." She studied his expression as she spoke. She wanted to discover that despite his colorful past, he had some decency in him.

If not, she had best sleep with one eye open and her shotgun at the ready, or he might take the animals and leave her stranded out here. She had to be ready for anything.

17

Cabot Falls, Vermont
Present Day

*S*ofia was ready. The desserts were baked. The bistro tables and chairs were ready to be distributed on the sidewalk and on the street where the square would be cordoned off for pedestrians on Founder's Day.

Construction workers were at work restoring Norton's storefront, although Sofia doubted there would be many people exercising that day. The machines had been removed and locked away at the police evidence warehouse at the edge of town.

Sofia dialed the number on the card the fire inspector had given her. She wanted her to know that she had detected burn gel and that Keeler was obviously lying about his injury.

"I appreciate your input, Mrs. Parker. Please leave the investigation to us. It could be dangerous. He is on our list of persons of interest. Beyond that, I can tell you nothing."

Frowning, Sofia hung up the phone. Gina and Jack would be arriving at the inn shortly. She had been so busy stocking up on desserts for the shop that she had thought little about anything else.

"Sofia, you don't have to feed them, so stop worrying," Jim told her. "They are coming to the Founder's Day celebration, and that means they expect to get hot dogs and burgers and barbecue on the square and finish off with your great desserts. Nobody is expecting you to do more than run your shop."

"I guess, but you know me. I hear that company's coming, and I fire up the oven and whip out the pasta. It's the Italian in me."

Her phone rang. It was Gina. "I can hardly wait to see everyone, especially Bryce. Every email from him has been filled with excited news. We're settled into the suite, complete with a big basket of fruit and cheese. That must have been your doing. They have such high praise for my little sister. I'm heading your way to help you get ready and to bring the badge . . . along with a surprise."

"Thanks." Sofia was grateful for the help. "But what's the surprise?"

"Now if I told you, it wouldn't be a surprise, would it? I'll be there soon."

It wasn't long before Gina and Jack were at the side door. "Vanessa took all the kids to the movies," Sofia said after greeting them. "The theater is showing some old movies about pioneers all week. I didn't think you'd get here so soon, or I'm sure Bryce would have been here."

Gina laughed. "I tend to doubt that, Sofia. He keeps telling me that he's never had such a great time. How can I help? Mix? Decorate? Pack? What?"

"Everything is pretty well ready, but we do need to pack it all up. But first show me the badge you found in the costume jewelry."

"Jack has it."

Jack pulled two items in handkerchiefs from his pocket. "Here is the Pinkerton badge." He unwrapped one and placed it carefully in Sofia's hand.

Sofia felt her breath catch. She closed her eyes. "Gina, do you realize that this is nearly 150 years old? Just think, it was worn by one of the first female detectives in the world, and she was our ancestor! But what else do you have?"

"Surprise!" Gina said. She placed a small pin in Sofia's hand. "Just look!"

"Secret Service?" Sofia read. "She joined the Secret Service? Is that why she disappeared after 1870? I was afraid she'd died in the Great Chicago Fire."

Gina shrugged. "I had no idea about the badge or who it belonged to. It was the only other such thing in Nonna's box."

"I looked it up, and it is authentic," Jack said. "The Secret Service was formed in 1865, and for a time, the Pinkertons *were* the Secret Service. In fact, President Lincoln actually hired the agency to provide for his personal safety during the Civil War."

"Why else would Nonna have had it?" Gina asked. "You know Jack is a history buff. He said that the first female Pinkerton agent was a woman named Kate Warne who was a spy during the war. Maybe Hannah was too."

"No, she was only a young teen during the war, and it appears she was living in an orphanage at that time," Sofia said. She handed the badges back.

"I've been thinking," Gina said. "The badges. They belong together. What if I get one of those shadow boxes for them? It would make a great display, and they belong with the quilt." Gina smiled at her younger sister. "They belong with you."

"I . . . I don't know what to say, Gina."

"You're doing a good thing, Sofia, researching the family history. I am so proud of you." Gina paused. "Now let's get to work before we both start to blubber."

They had nearly finished packing up Sofia's wares when Sofia and Gina's father called. "I found another Bible packed away that belonged to the Vincent Benetti family. A Georgina and Vincent Benetti. They list their marriage as 1839 in Vermont. A daughter, Angelique, was born in 1841 and a son, Zane, in '45. There is a penny postcard advertising milk and cheese with a Benetti Dairy Farm, and an affidavit signed by a Lydia Oaks that says she knew Hannah Reed from birth and her true birthday was August 2."

Before Sofia had a chance to digest what she'd just heard, the doorbell rang. It was a process server. Norton was suing her for destroying his business. She was summoned to go to court in two weeks. It was like throwing gasoline on a fire.

Greentown, Montana
Autumn 1871

Hannah fed the fire that Zane—masquerading as the grizzled prospector Porcupine—had built, while he gathered brush and twigs and laid them in a wide circle around them. When he had finished, he sat cross-legged on the ground opposite her. Zane showed not even a flicker of change in those emerald-green eyes as she told him about Partridge's daughter. She shifted her position under his steady gaze. *Does he understand how mesmerizing he is?*

The mountainous horizon was a faint glow that faded fast to purple. The moon at the far side shimmered like a pearl. Hannah startled at a distant sound; there was something eerie and feral about it. She shivered involuntarily. "What was that?"

"Coyote, from the sound of it," he replied with no sense of urgency.

Moments later, the same sound came from behind her. "Echo?"

"No, it's the other side of a conversation. The first one said, 'I'm lonely. Is anyone out there?' And the second one answered, 'I'm lonely too. Let's meet.'"

"Why, that's rather romantic of you, Porcupine," Hannah mused. The two sounds repeated but louder. Then sirenlike wails came from every direction. Hannah smiled. "It sounds as if they have a whole family. What are they saying now?"

"They said, 'There are two humans. It's time for a picnic.'"

"Oh, you're disgusting." The spell was broken. "What will we do?"

The horses whinnied, shaking their heads, ears pinned back. The mule brayed.

"I'll take care of it, Miss Jenkins."

Hannah felt her skin crawl up her arms as the sounds grew nearer and came from all sides. "Do you really think they can't step over those sticks?"

Zane set the circle of brush afire. "Now they won't."

Moments later, yellow eyes glowed beyond the fire ring.

"They'll get tired in a little while and look for their natural prey," he told her. "Take the tent. I'll stay out here and make sure the fire doesn't die down."

"I was foolish enough to come out here unprepared. It's your tent. You take it," Hannah said, despite desperately wanting it for herself.

He narrowed his eyes at her. "Why are you so stubborn?"

"I'm determined, not stubborn, Porcupine. It's how I learned to survive."

"Then the tent will remain empty." His mouth was a tight, thin line.

"Who's stubborn now?" Hannah mumbled as she spread the saddle blanket close to the fire and rested her head on the saddle as she saw him do. "Fine," she said.

"Fine," he repeated. He mumbled something else.

"What did you say?" she asked.

"I said, 'Stubborn woman!'" He turned his back to the fire and to her.

Hannah's mouth spread in a satisfied grin. She took a perverse pleasure in causing him a little frustration for a change. Being bullheaded was how she had kept her dignity all those years when everything from her orphan's uniform to people's attitudes told her that she was nothing and nobody. And being stubborn was how she had had the tenacity to become a Pinkerton. Yet she had a good feeling about this man, this enigma in her life. It was as if she didn't have to do everything for herself when he was around. Hannah wasn't sure she was completely comfortable with that idea. But for the moment, it was nice. She drifted into sleep, watching the flames of the campfire.

When she awoke, the coyotes had gone and the ring of fire was only smoldering ashes. The animals were grazing peacefully. The tent was down. And the aroma of coffee and beans made her nose quiver in anticipation. She stretched out the kinks she'd collected from sleeping on the hard ground.

Porcupine, aka Zane, aka the Gentleman Bandit, handed her a cup of coffee, which she eagerly drank. He offered her a tin plate with beans and hardtack. She pulled the jerky from her pack and offered it to him. They ate in silence.

Zane saddled their horses and packed his mule. He kicked dirt on the fire until it was out, scattered the remaining kindling, and buried the empty can.

"Thank you for your hospitality, Porcupine," she said. She could see a formation of hills that resembled one of the last sketches Partridge had made.

"We're going the same way. We may as well travel together. Safety in numbers," he said.

"Weren't you going the opposite way when we met? Besides, I can take care of myself. It isn't necessary." Hannah instantly regretted saying that. "I would not be upset if you decided to accompany me, however." She could feel his eyes on her. Why did he have to look at her that way?

"I guess I'm going whichever way you are."

After they had been underway for a few minutes, Zane broke

the silence. "Tell me about yourself, Miss Jenkins. For instance, why do you keep looking at those papers? Is that a map?"

Hannah momentarily froze. Perhaps he was hoping to get a look at the drawings. Once he got them, he might even leave her out here. But she dismissed that thought. He could have stolen the papers while she slept. No, he had something else up his sleeve. But what?

As her horse ambled along, she felt comfortable enough to loop the reins over the saddle horn and shuffle through the papers. Yes, her memory had served her right. There was the object of the last drawing. "This is where we say goodbye, Porcupine," she said. She turned her horse toward the now-familiar landscape—a row of mountains with tops that looked like ocean waves, and at their base, a stand of trees.

"You're heading the wrong way," he said matter-of-factly.

"I know what I'm doing." She knew there was an edge to her voice, but how dare he say that? She had the sketches. Had he seen them while she slept?

"You'll be wasting a whole day. Those mountains are at least twenty-five miles away. Distance fools you out here. Check that map you're so afraid I'll see."

Hannah's lips tightened into a thin, straight line. Impulsively, she shoved the drawing toward him. "Look at this, and then look there!" What a self-assured know-it-all he was!

"Think about it a minute, Miss . . . Jenkins. If that is where Partridge sat sketching something, would he draw what he was in the middle of, or would he—"

"Partridge? How did you know—" But then, suddenly, she felt so foolish. "Of course, he'd sketch what he was looking at." How she hated it when Zane was right and she was wrong. Some detective she'd turned out to be! "But how did you know even before I showed you the sketch?"

He pointed to the ground. "See that stick braced on top of the Y-shaped stick protruding from the ground?"

Hannah recognized the formation from one of Partridge's sketches on his letter. She had thought it was the results of restless hen-scratching while he thought of what to write.

"It's a sign the natives use to mark a trail for others to follow. The long stick points in the direction to go, and whether it is a long or short stick tells you the expected length of the journey. I've been seeing these since we left camp this morning."

"That's all very interesting, but Partridge is an easterner, not a native," she said.

"If he'd been out here long enough, he'd probably befriended some of the natives who traded with Green."

She looked at Talltree's map, and the claim did show it was opposite the scene Partridge had sketched. "Then I best be on my way," Hannah said. "Goodbye . . . and thank you—Porcupine."

She turned her horse in the direction of the stick. A minute later, she turned in her saddle to see that he had continued in their original direction. Hannah felt torn between relief and a feeling of loneliness as strong as the one she'd felt the day the orphanage door shut behind her.

It was hours before she came to what looked like a hole in the side of the mountain. A crude hand-painted sign read Talltree Mine—Keep Out. Hannah dismounted and tethered the reins to the sign. She spotted among the weeds several weathered boards nailed together and kicked them over. It was a sign that read Penny Partridge Mine: No Trespassing. It had a little partridge under the wing of a larger one.

This did not look hopeful for Mr. Partridge. Hannah returned to the mouth of the tunnel, where she found a leather pouch with candles, matches, and a spike holder. She stuck a candle in the holder and lit it, carefully stepping over and around the loose rocks as she crept deeper into the cave. Jagged outcroppings on the cave walls cast distorted shadows, and the air was stifling.

At the sound of shifting stones, she turned toward the sound in time to see the silhouette of a man. "Porcu—"

Two firm hands on her shoulders sent her hurling into a pit. Her head connected with the bottom, and everything faded to dark.

Her head hurt, and every muscle in her body felt stiff and on fire. She gradually moved. A sharp pain shot through her right ankle as she tried to stand, and she dropped to her knees. It throbbed miserably, but it was probably a sprain. She assured herself that nothing was broken—nothing except her pride, anyway. She should never have trusted that man. Just when she had begun to think that she had seen goodness in him, he had to do something like this.

"Hello?" she called out. If he had intended to kill her, why hadn't he done it last night? Had he enjoyed playing games with her emotions?

Her pragmatism and survival instincts kicked in. "First, I need light," she muttered, still trying to clear the fog from her mind. She remembered that she had been holding a lighted candle and the pouch when she was shoved. She crawled around the pit, feeling for the pouch. Her fingers came into contact with candle. Retrieving from her pocket the box of matches Porcupine had given her, she lit the candle again.

As her eyes adjusted to the dim light, Hannah jerked back as a chill crawled up her spine. She was not alone.

18

Cabot Falls, Vermont
Present Day

Sofia waved the court summons as she fumed. "I can't believe this! What is that man thinking? He knows very well that Inspector O'Leary said that someone had come down through the attic and started the fire on my side of the wall. Oh, I wish I'd never heard of the shop!"

"Sofia, it's just a tactic," Jack said. "You've heard the saying that the best defense is a good offense. He must realize that he's a prime suspect. He's only doing this to take the attention off himself."

"But a lawyer? Jack, I've put everything into the preparation for the shop. How can I afford to hire a lawyer?" Sofia sank into a chair, devastated.

"Our states have reciprocal privileges to practice law, so I'll represent you pro bono, but I doubt it will come to a trial. I predict that Norton will either be smart enough to drop the suit or he'll be under arrest before that date."

"But your campaign, Jack—"

"You're family, Sofia. Family is first always. Besides, the election is still months away."

The door burst open, and Bryce was first through the door. He hugged his parents warmly, all the while telling them about camping and visiting the newspaper and how he'd helped Matthew write a presentation for council. "We'll go to the committee the day before Founder's Day. Can you watch, huh, Dad?"

Gina threw her hands up. "I feel as if I'm meeting someone else's son! You look so . . . so . . . ."

"Comfortable," Bryce said.

Vanessa was the last to enter. "Look who I found just pulling up." Sofia was delighted to see her father.

"Dad! I thought you weren't coming until Founder's Day," Sofia said.

"Oh, an hour's drive isn't all that much. I'm going back after a while. I got all excited about the things I found and wanted to get them to you. It looks as if before she died, your mother had started some research on this Hannah Reed. She didn't get very far, but what she found could be a help, I hope."

He handed Sofia a loose-leaf notebook with items in plastic sheets. One was a letter of commendation to Hannah Reed written on Pinkerton Agency stationery.

Sofia read it aloud:

> *For your exemplary work in not only bringing crimi-nals to justice, but also in clearing the innocent, you have earned the gratitude of the entire agency. We will miss your service but wish you well in your forthcoming marriage.*

It was signed by Allan Pinkerton. There was also a certificate naming her a member of the Female Detective Bureau signed by Kate Warne.

"Those documents prove what we already suspected, Dad, and it sounds like she left the agency to get married, but—"

"There's more. See this copy of a Chicago newspaper article that mentioned Lydia Oaks? It says she was the manager of the Allison Johnson Home for Indigent Women, established in 1871."

Sofia snapped her fingers. "Allison Johnson—A.J. Those are the initials on the square. But what has that got to do with Hannah Reed? And who is Allison Johnson to us? The more we learn, the more confusing it gets."

Gina patted Sofia's arm. "I'm sure you'll figure it out, Sofia. Everything is going to work out just fine. Nonna always said *Il cuor non sbaglia*: Trust your instincts. The heart sees farther than the head. You see with your heart, and it hasn't failed you yet."

Sofia smiled. Even if some of that was only sweet talk to keep her working on the research, it was nice to hear from Gina.

She felt like her life was a cluster of little containers—family, the frantic baking for Founder's Day, and the crazy problems with Norton. Even when Founder's Day was over and she could close up the shop and move on, that man was going to be next door to her. It was as if he had edged his way into every facet of her life. He was a human monkey wrench!

Why couldn't Inspector O'Leary and Officer Quimby find the proof to lock that man away? So he was in custody when one of the fires started. What about his garage? He had no real reason for all that lighter fluid. And wasn't that where the fire started?

Yet he had said, "They tried to kill me." She knew instinctively that Keeler was in on it. She was sure that the cast he wore was just to hide the burn he must have sustained when he started those fires. Why hadn't Norton said "he" instead of "they"? Was there a third person—and if so, who?

Sofia tried to think the way she imagined Hannah might. *Who would have the most to gain from these fires?*

Outskirts of Greentown, Montana
Autumn 1871

Who? Hannah drew a jagged breath, which caught in her throat. She stared at the decomposing body of Penny Patridge's father. For a moment Hannah forgot her precarious situation. Her heart ached for Penny. The gold ring on his finger must've been specially made, because it had a relief of a small partridge.

He had probably been pushed, just as she had. The thought brought her back to reality. The sides of the pit were too high to climb without help. She could perish down here.

"Well, that isn't going to happen," Hannah said. She lit more candles and found the metal candleholder, which she used to dig into the hard wall. "I will not just lie down and die." The soft metal bent against the hard sides of the pit, but she continued plunging it with as much force as she could.

She heard shifting rocks above.

"Hannah! Hannah! Are you all right?"

She recognized the voice. It was Zane. He'd called her by her real name, not "Miss Jenkins." "Help! Get me out of here!"

"I'll get a rope!"

She heard the shifting of stones and then silence—deadly silence. It seemed to last forever. Just when she feared she had been abandoned, a rope slid along the wall within reach. "Can you slip the loop around you? Pull it snug." His voice was so calm that Hannah did as he instructed.

The rope went taut. Hannah held firmly as she was lifted to the surface, where Zane wrapped his arms around her, pulling her to him. "Hannah." She could feel his breath near her ear. The throaty whisper was so tender and full of relief that it took her breath away. She had never heard her name said that way. A flood of conflicting emotions bombarded her—joy, fear, affection, and contentment. She melted against his chest, silently shedding a few tears.

As suddenly as he had grabbed her, he gently pushed her away. "Can you walk on your own?" He seemed to grow distant right before her eyes. Had he come to his senses and realized that he'd used her real name?

Confused by the sudden change, she was reminded that he was her adversary. "Yes." She tried to walk, but lightning bolts of pain shot through her ankle, and she felt herself falling.

Zane scooped her into his arms and carried her into the sunlight where he set her on the ground.

"Go, Zane. You mustn't stay; I'd have to honor my oath and arrest you if you don't go. Please!" Momentarily blinded by the bright sunlight, she blinked rapidly. Hannah's eyes adjusted, and she stared in disbelief. On the ground, a man was writhing and wiggling, muttering through a bandana that gagged him. His hands were tied together behind his back and attached by a rope to his ankles.

"Josiah Talltree—your prisoner, Hannah," Zane said. "I caught him about to let your horse go and figured he was up to no good."

"You followed me?"

"Let's just say that we were traveling in the same direction. I was a little behind, that's all."

"Well, I'm grateful you did. You're not some kind of guardian angel, are you?" She rubbed her rapidly swelling ankle.

Zane laughed. "No, hardly. Just a man."

Hannah couldn't stop a smile from spreading across her face. She thought he was much more than that, although she wasn't sure what just yet. "I found Partridge's body in the pit. I figure that Talltree got rid of him the same way he tried to get rid of me, and then he staked the claim for himself. I'll get him back to Dry Gulch and give Miss Partridge the bad news. If you'll tie that scoundrel to his horse, I'll do the rest. And then you need to disappear, maybe change your name. I don't want to see you again." She wished she could take that back. She would miss him terribly.

"I'm not going anywhere but back to Dry Gulch with you and this murdering thief." Zane's gaze was focused totally on her. "First, let me see about that ankle."

Hannah kept silent as he tore a strip from his shirt and bound her ankle. "Thank you, Zane. Now go. I don't want to arrest you—not now, not ever." The quiet way he'd spoken her name earlier still echoed in her mind.

Zane raked the gray wig from his head and tugged off the beard. "Maybe it's time to introduce myself, Hannah." He reached into his back pocket and pulled out a silver shield. "Agent Zane Benetti."

"Secret Service?" Hannah stared. "But the train robbery—"

"It was a ruse to be accepted into the gang. We needed to know where their hideout was or we might have searched those hills forever. We didn't want to go after them around passengers for fear some innocents would be hurt. Clerks in our agency have already reimbursed the victims and apologized."

Hannah wrapped her fingers around the locket. "I thought you'd been killed with them. You returned my locket. You knew I was a Pinkerton?"

"Not then," he said. "Not until I saw you in Dry Gulch."

"Then . . . why?"

"Think about it, Hannah." His eyes seemed to dance with mischief.

"I have thought about it," she admitted. "A lot." She thought about his eyes too, emerald pools that she felt she could fall into and drown. The stranger with the Romanesque nose, strong, square jawline, and beautiful smile had haunted her dreams. Blushing, she dismissed the thought.

"I was smitten the moment I saw you," he confessed. "That defiant stubborn chin . . . I could see that the locket meant a great deal to you. I didn't want you for one moment to think that it was gone forever. Maybe you'll tell me about it one day."

Hannah dipped her head, suddenly feeling shy. "Maybe." Had he just said "smitten"? With her? "But why didn't you tell me in Dry Gulch? We're on the same side, you know." It felt good to realize that.

Zane laughed. "It's the Secret Service, Hannah. The operative word here is *secret*. I wasn't sure if I'd need my gambler disguise a little longer. Besides, I just couldn't resist having a bit of fun with a fiery Irish redhead."

"Irish? You think I'm Irish?" Hannah asked. She hadn't really thought about that. She had always considered herself just plain Hannah. Perhaps she'd know soon enough.

"What else would you be with titian hair and eyes the color of a cloudless sky?" he asked. "I guess maybe a Scottish lass." He helped her to her feet.

She clung to his arm unsteadily. "And now, Agent Benetti, if you'll tie Talltree to his horse, I need to get him to Dry Gulch and deliver the bad news to Miss Partridge. I'll send someone back to recover her father's body. I'll be all right from here."

Zane wrapped his arms around her and lifted her to her horse. With his hand lingering on the small of her back, he said, "I haven't the slightest doubt that you would be, Hannah. But this *was* my assignment. Partridge contracted with the Treasury to sell any and all silver he discovered. He'd sent a map with his final missive, and then there was no further word. I was sent to investigate."

He easily lifted Talltree to his horse and tied him securely to the saddle. Handing the reins to Hannah, he said, "Your prisoner, ma'am." He pulled out a compass. "If you follow me, we can cut off a day's travel."

In Greentown, they modified the stolen claim to indicate that Penny Partridge was the rightful owner. Then they escorted Talltree to Dry Gulch. After visiting Miss Partridge with the news of her father's death and the mine he'd left her, Hannah and Zane telegraphed their respective agencies and sat down to await replies.

Zane leaned his chair back on two legs and shoved his hat forward to shade his eyes.

Smiling contentedly, Hannah studied his profile, thinking he'd dropped off to sleep. She startled when he spoke.

"What's your next step, Hannah? You plan on staying with Pinkerton's?"

"Yes, it's what I do. But I plan on taking some time off; I have something important to do first. What else would I do?"

He leaned forward and shoved his hat back. "Oh, you know—marriage, children, family." His emerald eyes darkened to shamrock. She noticed a slight tic at one corner of his mouth.

Family. The word stabbed at her heart like a sharp knife. How could she even think of family until she knew who she was and where she came from? Was he testing her? "What about you, Zane? You must have someone waiting for you back home, wherever that is." She held her breath.

His thoughts seemed to be elsewhere for a moment as he looked away. At last, he turned to her, grinning. "There's Bessie and Lou Lou and Rachel. They're milk cows. My folks have a dairy farm in Vermont, but they want to retire whenever I can get back there and run it."

"A dairy farm? Somehow I can't imagine an adventurous man like you settling down to milk cows, Zane."

"And make cheese," he added, smiling wistfully. "There's a brook running through the fields, and if you listen carefully, the water makes music as it rushes over the stones. That's where I built my house, with a porch that runs the length of the front and around the sides so that you can see the moon wherever it is."

Hannah closed her eyes, imagining it. "It sounds wonderful. Whatever made you leave it for this life?" The silence was so long that she wondered if he would answer.

His expression morphed into a scowl. "The war, Hannah; I went to war. When it was over, things had changed. People had changed." He exhaled deeply.

Hannah studied his handsome face, so clouded by an unnamed hurt. Someone who hadn't waited as she had promised? So he, too, had experienced the pain of abandonment. "But you'll go back to it eventually, right?"

"Not yet, Hannah. Not until I can take a bride who is willing to settle into a quiet life and chase children instead of criminals."

He looked at her so intently that she felt as if he could see into her very soul. How she longed to tell him that she recognized that need because she had it too. But part of his job was pretending he was someone else. It was her job too. How would either of them ever know what was real and what was pretend?

Hannah shifted uncomfortably. Why did he have to look at her like that? She opened her mouth to speak, but the telegraph machine suddenly clattered to life. The clerk hastily scribbled on a pad. Before he could transcribe it, a second missive clattered in.

The clerk wore a stunned expression as he handed them the messages. Hannah read in disbelief.

GOOD JOB STOP NEED YOU HOME STOP CHICAGO ON FIRE STOP ALL AGENTS REPORT STOP

Hannah looked up from her message to see Zane's grim expression. He knew. She burst into tears. "Oh, Zane. The orphanage! The children! What if—"

Zane wrapped his arms around her, pulling her to him. "Shh, Hannah, don't cry. We'll find them. We'll make sure that they are okay. We'll do it together."

Stunned, the two walked back to the hotel without another word. Hannah packed in a daze, her cheeks wet with tears. They would go together on the train, but that would be the end of it. Like her, he had trouble trusting. Unless they could honestly tell each other about their pasts, there could be no trust. Without trust, there could be no future.

Hannah sighed wearily. Soon enough, she would be back on her own in Chicago, or what was left of it. She would go wherever the agency sent her. She would be whoever she had to be. Zane would either go on missions or return to Vermont, assuming he found the bride he was looking for. Perhaps their paths would cross again, or perhaps not. *A dairy farm, of all things.* She'd never even seen a cow up close. Did she dare even imagine?

She folded the red bandana and placed it in a corner of the luggage. The peppermint aroma had vanished. Perhaps her memories of the dashing Agent Zane Benetti would too.

Enough of that, she berated herself. She shuddered, thinking of her city. How had the fire started? So many of the buildings were constructed from wood. It must have been a tinderbox. She prayed that Greta had gotten the children to safety. Perhaps they had sought refuge in the lake. Had her boardinghouse and all those loving, caring people survived?

On the train ride to Chicago, she and Zane sat together. But he had constructed an invisible wall between them, shutting her out. Were his thoughts on the Chicago fire? Or was it something else? Who had hurt him so deeply?

19

Cabot Falls, Vermont
Present Day

*H*er future was the last thing on her mind as Sofia pulled her black dress with the empire waistline from her closet. It had been quite a while since she'd had an occasion to wear it. With the string of pearls Jim had given her as a wedding gift and the little pearl earrings she had found at a rummage sale, it should look suitable for dinner at the Cabot Inn. The McCrays were hosting the entire Parker brood this evening.

Satisfied that everyone looked their Sunday best, she set the alarm code and joined them in the Suburban for the short ride to the inn. As many pies and cakes as she had baked for the inn, she rarely had the chance to enjoy their cuisine except on special occasions. It was an excellent diversion from her worries over the lawsuit and the celebration.

Midmeal, Sofia dropped a piece of her filet mignon on her lap. "Oh my. You just can't take me anywhere," she said, laughing, and excused herself. In the powder room, she quickly blotted, spot-cleaned, and turned on the blow dryer. Two women standing at the mirror chatted with each other as they primped, ignoring Sofia's drama.

"Mark promised me that we're going to the Caymans. We might even live there awhile," the ash blonde said.

"Live there! What will become of your real estate business?"

The dark-haired woman laughed. "The Caymans. Isn't that where people go to hide money and avoid arrest? You aren't keeping secrets, are you, Ruth Keeler?"

"Shh, Sue. I wasn't supposed to tell anyone."

The two of them left. When Sofia was satisfied that she looked presentable, she returned to her table. She could see the two women seated two tables over with Mark Keeler and Wilson Watson.

"You are suddenly quiet, Sofia," Gina said. "Is everything all right?"

"I'm not sure. I'll tell you later if I figure it out," Sofia replied.

They saw the McCrays to their suite and then headed for the parking garage. As they got off the elevator, loud voices erupted. It was Keeler and the banker, Watson. All Sofia heard was the banker shouting that he would not be left behind to clean up the mess.

"That's what Norton's for!" the other man yelled.

When the Parkers came into their view, the two men quickly parted, climbed into their vehicles, and drove out of the garage.

On the way home, Sofia asked Jim, "Could a real estate agent, a banker, and a property owner make a profit if that property were destroyed?"

"I suppose so, if the property was overvalued and overinsured, but it would take a conspiracy of lies to pull it off," Jim said. "What are you thinking?"

"What if it was not just one property but lots of them?"

"Then I imagine the amount of combined money would be significant," Jim said. "Sofia, are you on to something? If so, tell Officer Quimby or Inspector O'Leary. You stay out of it."

"Don't worry, sweetheart. Nobody ever got in trouble in the library archives. I want to check something out before I raise any alarms."

Back at home, Sofia gave Fergus the remaining filet and said good night to the kids. She left Jim reading and went to the basement to check her computer. A little family research might help her stop thinking about her suspicions about Keeler and Watson.

She looked on a genealogical website for more information about Lydia Oaks. Before she managed the charity home, she had been listed in the household of Mrs. Temperance Throckmorton Grey. It was the same address as the women's home. It was unusual for a woman in that era to use her name like that; she must have been wealthy. Further research showed she had a daughter who had died quite young. The only connection between this Grey woman and Hannah Reed was Lydia Oaks. Sofia understood that information might be sketchy about Hannah, because as an undercover agent, she would have kept her life outside the agency private. But surely this Oaks woman left a bigger footprint on history, as would her employer.

Could Allison Johnson be the deceased daughter of Temperance? Sofia yawned as the full meal and drowsiness took effect. *Tomorrow*, she told herself. Tomorrow would be soon enough. They would all attend the village council meeting in support of Matthew and Bryce and their presentation. Then she'd get Gina to research the genealogy collection of articles at the library while she remained at the village hall to see if her hunch was right before she told Officer Quimby what she'd overheard.

There was an old saying about birds of a feather flocking together. And she'd seen Norton, Keeler, and Watson huddled together a lot of late. If she was right, there would be not one arrest but three. Whatever proof she could find, she needed to find it quickly before one or more of them fled to a country without an extradition policy.

"That's what Norton's for," Keeler had said. What did he mean by that? Was Norton a sacrificial lamb in this plot? If he was somehow a reluctant part of it, could he be innocent? She couldn't get Norton's words out of her thoughts: *They tried to kill me.* And the look on his face that night had been one of pure fear.

She dismissed the thought. She couldn't imagine an innocent person being as vicious as Norton. Had she misread him?

Chicago, Illinois
Autumn 1871

She had misread Zane, Hannah decided. "Smitten" was hardly a lifetime commitment. She shoved thoughts of him aside as the train pulled into Chicago. Hannah stared out the window. A major portion of downtown was simply gone. In its place were blackened rubble and the horrible stench of charred debris. People, their faces expressionless with shock, picked through the remnants of their lives in the squandered hope that they might find a photograph of a loved one or anything from life before the fire.

Hannah moaned pitifully. "This is awful. Simply awful."

Zane clasped her elbow. "I'll see if there is any transportation in operation."

"I want to check on the children first. Then I'll need to see about the boardinghouse before I see Mr. Pinkerton. But you don't have to—"

His voice was firm, almost sharp. "I said we'd do it together. Let someone help, Hannah. You don't have to do everything alone."

She nodded wordlessly, grateful for the company. He located a carriage, and she gave him the address. Hannah let her breath out in a relieved sigh as the destruction ended blocks away from the building. The church stood unharmed too. As the carriage stopped in front of the orphanage, the door burst open, and girls spilled onto the sidewalk, shouting her name and rushing to hug her.

Greta stood at the door, smiling. She assured Hannah that they were fine and needed nothing. "Hannah, you look so grand. I'm so glad to see that you are doing well. The girls have read and reread *Little Women*. Wait just a minute." She left and returned with an envelope. "They did this letter for you, but I didn't know where to send it." She peered over Hannah's shoulder. "Your fellow is quite handsome, Hannah."

Hannah accepted the envelope with her name on it. "Oh, he's not my fellow." Her words caught in her throat. "He is just a—a friend." She hugged Greta and each of the girls. It felt strange to walk away from the orphanage again. She wiped a tear that lingered on her cheek.

Zane took her hand and helped her back into the carriage. "Those children are fond of you, Hannah. I can see that."

"It was my home for eighteen years, Zane. Hannah Reed isn't even my real name. Greta gave it to me when I arrived there only a few days old. I don't know who I am." She felt lighter now that she'd told him. But how would he feel about that?

He gazed at her silently for so long that she felt as if her world were closing in, squeezing the life out of her. "Hannah." It was that breathless tone she'd heard in the mine. "Hannah, what do you mean, you don't know who you are? What does a name have to do with it? I see a beautiful woman who is stubbornly self-reliant but eager to help everyone else. It's what makes you good at your job."

Hannah looked away. *Good at my job.* Sometimes she supposed she was. And if that was destined to be her life, then so be it. "I'm a pig in a poke, an unknown, so I can easily be anybody I want, like the Chameleon who trained me." Anyone but the person she really wanted to be. "Never mind. I need to check on the boardinghouse."

Here her worst fears came to fruition. The house was in ruins. A lone figure was hunched over, poking at the scattered debris with a stick. Hannah recognized the building janitor as she scrambled from the carriage with Zane close behind. "Mr. Ambrose!"

The man stopped and looked around. "Hannah! Oh, it's mighty good to see you, young lady. I'm sorry that your home-coming isn't what you expected."

"Did—did everyone make it out all right, Mr. Ambrose?"

"We did, my dear. Those little drills we hated to go through paid off. Some are with relatives. Others are scattered about. Oh, I almost forgot." He reached into a large leather bag. "I'm sorry I couldn't save it all, but I knew how much it meant to you." He handed her a square of charred pink silk. It was the corner of the quilt that bore the initials A.J. and the letters she thought were gibberish.

Hannah touched it to her cheek. It smelled of smoke. "Perfect, Mr. Ambrose." She hugged him and turned to leave, and she saw Zane standing at the walk. His silhouette was so tall and straight that she felt her heart skip a beat. There was the faintest smile on his lips, and his intent gaze was riveted on her. What could he be thinking?

"This remnant of a pink quilt and my locket are my only clues to my real family," she told Zane. "My mother left me at the orphanage. How can I ever hope to have a family of my own? What if I'm like her?" She searched his face for an expression that would tell her how he felt.

"Is that what you think? That you'd abandon your baby? Oh, Hannah, that is something I could never imagine you doing," Zane said.

"First, there's the fire investigation," she said. "And I need to report to Mr. Pinkerton." She offered her hand. "Thank you, Agent Zane Benetti, for everything, but I guess this is goodbye."

He stared at her hand as if he'd never seen one before. He inhaled deeply, letting his breath out in a soft sigh. "Yes, of course.

We have our jobs to do." He squeezed her hand. "Goodbye, Hannah Reed. I hope you find what you're looking for. Take the carriage. I'll get another."

As the carriage lumbered away, Hannah looked back to see Zane standing alone on the walkway. It was sad. After all they'd been through together, it shouldn't end like this. *But it's better this way.* So why didn't it feel better?

The Pinkerton offices had been spared. Hannah greeted everyone and turned in her handwritten reports on the cases that had kept her out West so long.

"Hannah, we have our operatives scattered around the burn area and among the refugee camps outside the city, gathering information and preventing looting," Mr. Pinkerton said. "But I'm glad you're back. A mansion several blocks over from the main fire burned to the ground, and there were casualties."

"Is that surprising?" Hannah asked, sliding into the chair across from his desk.

"Yes and no," Mr. Pinkerton said. "The fire was halted more than three blocks from the home. It's not impossible that embers were carried on the wind, skipping all the homes in between. Fires are freakish and unpredictable, but then you never know. Look into it. I trust your instincts."

Hannah took the address down. She took a carriage to the location. Sure enough, there was only rubble and the charred remains of furniture, bathtubs, and a sink. The properties were wide, and the mansions on either side of the burned home were still standing; they had suffered only heat blisters on the exterior paint.

She rang the bell at one of the neighboring homes and learned from the housemaid that an elderly woman, Bethel Grover, had owned the destroyed residence. Her daughter, Josephine, had married Jefferson Lethbridge, and the two lived with her, as did her son, Reginald.

She read the report that Mr. Pinkerton had given her. *Three casualties. Two females and one male. That means that one male must've survived, but which one?* The coroner had been over-whelmed with fire victims. It was impossible to estimate when they would be able to tell her anything about the victims from this fire.

Hannah asked the housemaid what she knew about the family. Reluctantly, the woman told her that Mrs. Grover had been unhappy that her daughter married Lethbridge, who referred to himself as an inventor, although he didn't seem to invent anything and he basically lived off his mother-in-law's wealth. The elderly woman was bedridden. The maid didn't know much about her son except that she saw him leave in the mornings and return in the evenings, so she'd assumed he worked.

Hannah thanked her for her help and walked over to the ruins. Might the son be the missing person? Whichever person survived and for whatever reason, he would be a wealthy man now—unless, of course, he had taken advantage of the downtown fire to kill off his family. She stood amidst the charred remains, studying the scene. One bathtub protruded grotesquely from pipes that held it in place upstairs. There were remnants of stairs that had once led to the second floor. A sink and second tub indicated where the kitchen and an additional bath had been. The brick fireplace was still standing, but it had been converted to gas, with a heating element installed in the firebox.

She bent over to examine the soot-covered valve. It was in the open position. No freak embers had ignited this fire. It was murder. Hannah had started to stand when she felt a sharp blow to the back of her head, and darkness settled over her.

"Hannah . . . Hannah, my love." Zane's voice was distant, but his words were clear.

She smiled groggily. "Umm, such a nice dream. Please don't wake me up," she murmured. "Yes, dear Zane, I love you too."

"Hannah, wake up. Are you all right? Talk to me, Hannah. Can you see me?"

"Oh, my head! Someone hit me." She groaned, trying to focus her eyes on the figure leaning over her, cradling her in strong arms. Those gorgeous emerald eyes looked back at her. She reached up and cupped his face in her hand. It felt warm and pliant, but solid, not a dream. "Zane?" He was real. Had what she heard been real or part of her dream? She jerked her hand back, leaving a sooty smudge on his face. "How did you find me?"

"I checked with the office. Pinkerton told me where he had sent you. I must have arrived just in time."

She tried to sit up. "Oh! What hit me?" She searched his face for any clue that he'd actually murmured what she'd heard in her head.

"It was more who than what, I think," he said. His scowl softened, but there was no indication that he was more than concerned for her wellbeing.

"Yes, I remember now. I found the gas valve open and realized that this was murder," Hannah told him. A pain shot through her head and neck as she turned to look. The valve was now closed. "It appears that our murderer returned to the scene of the crime." She laughed despite the pain. "And left a perfect print. Look!" In the soot on the handle was a clear print of ridges and loops.

"The scoundrel won't get away," Zane said.

Hannah nodded. "If he hadn't come back to close that valve, I imagine all of his prints would have been wiped out by the fire."

Zane removed a pad of paper from Hannah's bag and pressed a sheet to the handle. When he removed it, he had a mirror replica of the thumbprint. "We need to get this to the office," he said.

"Whether it's the son or son-in-law, he will eventually be arrested. The proof is in the print."

"Let me see if I can get up now." With Zane's help, Hannah stood on wobbly legs.

"I'll see you safely back to headquarters," Zane said. "You're not very steady on your feet." Together they made their way back to the street and the carriage in which Zane had arrived.

The euphoria had vanished like mist. Perhaps she'd been mistaken. In her clouded state, she had only imagined the endearment. But what if she'd uttered her love out loud? *Did he hear me?* "I'm sure you have more important things to do, Agent Benetti."

His jaw tensed, and he turned suddenly forward and curtly gave the driver the Pinkerton address.

Hannah sighed wearily. They were both stubborn fools; neither of them was ready to risk the hurt of rejection again.

The fire had destroyed much of the city and probably all of its archives. What hope did she have of ever discovering the details of her true past now? No past and no future. She felt like flotsam on the wind. She needed to leave Chicago far behind.

20

Washington, D.C.
December 1871

*H*annah gazed out the window of the train. She clasped her hands together to keep them from shaking. She didn't want to think about today. She flashed back to last week, when Jefferson Lethbridge had arrived at the coroner's office to request death certificates; he'd pretended he'd been out of town and was devastated to hear of his family's demise. She'd arrested him, and when she confronted him with the thumbprint and the scenario of murder, he'd confessed. Case closed. It was a satisfying feeling, bringing a criminal to justice, speaking for those who could no longer speak for themselves.

She shifted in her seat, sighing wearily. It was a tiring journey, but one she had to make alone. Zane was called back to his headquarters in Washington, D.C. He had been angry with her and had left Chicago without saying goodbye. She missed him terribly. Why couldn't he understand? No matter how many characters he played as a secret agent, he always knew who he was; he knew he had a home to return to. Why couldn't he understand that she had none? Why couldn't he understand that without that, she had nothing to offer him but questions?

Hannah had believed that her last chance to know the truth about her past had vanished in the fire. With Mr. Pinkerton's blessing, she was taking leave of the agency to see if the duplicate archives in the nation's capital could be of help.

The Smithsonian Institution—established a few years before she was born—held an incredible amount of information: old newspapers, census records, and even personal letters. There was a small chance that she'd find what she needed.

"Hannah, be prepared for disappointment," Mr. Pinkerton had said. "What you're looking for may not be there. And if it is, you may not like what you find. We have no control over the past, only the future."

She felt she had no control over that, either. Mr. Pinkerton had said that he asked a friend to meet her. But how would she recognize him? When she asked, Mr. Pinkerton smiled and said, "Don't worry; he'll recognize you."

The train pulled into the depot with a hiss of steam, and Hannah grabbed her valise. When she stepped onto the platform, her jaw slacked in surprise. "Zane!" She could feel her breath catch in her throat. The very sight of him standing so tall and assured buoyed her spirits.

His lips curled into a wistful smile and those beautiful emerald eyes glittered. She half-expected—wanted—him to embrace her. Instead, he took her elbow. "This way, Hannah. Is that all the luggage you brought?"

She nodded, numb with disappointment. She had to hasten her pace to keep up with him as they walked to the waiting carriage. "I'd hoped to hear from you, Zane. Even a postcard to let me know—"

"Know what, Hannah? What should I say? 'Safe at headquarters. Having a wonderful time. Wish you were here'?"

Stunned, she said, "You're angry with me. Why?"

"Why? It's your obsession with your past, Hannah. Do you really think I care about that? Do you think I care what your birth name is? Who your mother is? Hannah, I . . . I . . . ."

Hannah was on the verge of tears. "It matters to *me*, Zane." How could she expect him to love her when she couldn't love herself?

"I promised Allan that I'd get you settled and then see if I could help with the research," he told her. "Unless, of course, you don't want me—"

"I do want you . . ." She gulped. "To help me," she finished.

They lunched in awkward silence in the dining hall of her hotel. Then he hailed a carriage for the short ride to the Smithsonian. With the help of a research assistant, they settled at a table with a large bound book, a collection of Chicago newspapers from 1840 to 1860.

"I was born in August 1849," Hannah said. "The only other thing I know is that I look a great deal like the woman in this locket and that I was wrapped in the pink quilt." She pulled the charred quilt remnant from her bag. "See? There are the initials A.J. and these other letters—*a ghrá mo chroí*—that make no sense. Maybe whoever embroidered them hadn't finished."

Zane took the square. "I know this. My grandmother was Irish; she always said this when she tucked me in. It's pronounced ah-graw-muh-KREE. It's Irish for 'love of my heart.' She even cross-stitched a sampler with it."

"Then why did I grow up in an orphanage, without love?" She flipped open the cover of the bound newspapers and was reaching to turn to papers from the year of her birth when Zane stopped her with his hand over hers.

"Before you look at this, look at me, Hannah," he told her. "Look hard. What do you see?"

What did she see? She saw the face she wanted to wake to for the rest of her life. She saw pain in his eyes. Did he still grieve for his lost love? "I see . . . I see the man who is always here for me, who . . . who—"

"The man who loves you, Hannah, no matter what you find

in here; that's who you see here. Even if you find nothing, it's you, the woman who made me trust again, believe in forever again, that I love."

She felt as if her heart would burst from happiness at those words. "Zane, I do love you—even more than I believed possible. Loving you—and you loving me—gives me the strength to move beyond whatever we discover. I just have to do this. I am a missing piece in search of a puzzle."

They spent the rest of the day in the newspaper archives. The research assistant pointed out that the quilt remnant was expensive silk and suggested they look through the social pages first. Photos were rarely reproduced in the papers at that time. One exception was the identical likeness in her locket. It was an announcement of the engagement of a Miss Allison Grey to Baron Liam Johnson of Ireland and England. The article explained that he was a descendant of nobility awarded a barony by Henry VIII upon their surrender after the war between Ireland and England.

She found the notice of their marriage in England, which took place some months later. Thereafter were printed a succession of mocking accounts in the news section that told of the "Baroness" Allison Johnson returning to her home in Chicago to await the birth of her child. According to those accounts, Liam Johnson was not a baron at all. In fact, he was penniless, and so far down the line of descendants that he'd never be a baron. He had arrived in Chicago, and he had established himself in its social circles where every ambitious mother seemed bent on her daughter becoming a baroness. The wealthy Mrs. Throckmorton Grey had been no different.

Allison, with her sizable trust fund, had won his heart. They had lived lavishly in England until her trust fund was empty. Much older than Allison, Liam had died of apoplexy soon after the money ran out. Allison Johnson, barely eighteen, had returned home in May, where she went into seclusion at the Grey mansion. Her obituary was published that August. There was no birth announcement.

Hannah looked up from the pages. "Zane, could this be my birthright? Is the A.J. for *Allison Johnson*? Am I a child of scandal?"

"We don't choose our parents, Hannah. If you want to see this through, we need to return to Chicago."

"We?" She liked the sound of it.

"Get used to it, Hannah. It is *we—you and me*—from now on, all right?"

Chicago, Illinois
Autumn 1871

Hannah stood on the walkway, staring at the huge brick mansion that rose like a fortress from behind thick bushes.

"Shall I go with you?" Zane asked. The tone in his voice told her that he already knew the answer.

"I need to do this alone," Hannah replied. "But I promise this is the last thing I ever want to do alone." She squeezed his hand reassuringly and then walked up the stone steps and knocked.

A slender, gray-haired woman opened the door. Her eyes seemed to roll back, and she crumpled to the floor in a faint. Hannah motioned for Zane, and the two of them settled the woman on a sofa in the parlor. Hannah found the kitchen and brought water back to bathe the woman's face.

"I—I thought for a moment that I was seeing a ghost. Except for your hair, you are the image of dear, sweet Allison," the woman said. "She named you Ann, you know. Ann Johnson."

Ann Johnson. Hannah let the name roll around in her thoughts. It was a stranger's name. She felt no kinship to it. "You're my grandmother?"

"Oh no, dear. I am Lydia Oaks. Mrs. Grey died many years ago. I was her housekeeper. She left the house in trust for the day you'd come. I stayed on as I promised, waiting." She cradled Hannah's face in her hands. "You came."

"I read about my mother—and my father—in old newspapers. I saw her obituary. It said she died of pneumonia. In August? What really happened?"

Lydia shook her head. "The scandal is what did it. The poor little thing grieved to death, I think. Mrs. Grey was a stubborn old aristocrat. She practically forced poor Allison into that marriage. All the socialites were hungry for those meaningless titles. It was a status thing, you know.

"Allison was a fragile young thing, physically as well as emotionally. She felt humiliated, but she did want you so much. When you were born with that beautiful red hair like your father's, Allison loved you immediately. When she died a few days later, Mrs. Grey went out of her mind. She said I had to take you to the church and leave you."

Lydia's cheeks were wet with tears. "I had to do it, Ann. This was no place for you. You reminded her every day of what she'd done to her daughter. I wrapped you in the quilt your mother made and put that locket with you, so you would know you were loved."

Hannah stood and inhaled deeply, letting her breath out slowly. "Thank you, Lydia." She took Zane's arm. "I'm ready. Let's go."

Lydia grabbed her hand. "Ann! This is all yours. Mrs. Grey came to hate herself for what she did. She left it to you."

Hannah patted her hand. "I don't want—" She stopped short

as an idea entered her thoughts. "How many rooms does this old mansion have?"

"It's six bedrooms, plus two more in the carriage house," Lydia replied.

"And the trust fund?" Hannah asked.

"Enormous, Ann."

"Throw back those drapes and let the sunshine in, Lydia. It should look welcoming, because it will be a place where women can live until they can stand on their own. Make that happen, Lydia."

Lydia's face spread into a smile. "Yes, the Ann Johnson Home for Women!"

"Make that the Allison Johnson Home," Hannah said. "Zane, now I'm ready."

Once they were outside, Zane pulled Hannah to a halt. "Do you mean it, Hannah—or should I call you Ann? Are you sure you are ready?"

"I am glad that I know what happened, but knowing doesn't change who I am. I know that now. I'm not Ann. I'm Hannah Reed, and I'm grateful to my grandmother."

Zane's eyebrows lifted. "Really?"

"Yes, because I grew up stronger than my mother." She paused before continuing. "And I might never have met you. More than anything, I want to be Hannah Benetti."

"You've had a pretty adventurous life with the Pinkertons, Hannah. Are you ready to give all that up for a dairy farmer in Vermont?"

Hannah laughed. "What? You mean give up being whacked on the head, shoved into a pit, and left to die? Oh yes, I'll really miss that! Besides, I have a feeling that life with Zane Benetti will always be an adventure."

Zane wrapped his arms around her and pulled her to him. "Hannah."

She smiled contentedly. How she loved hearing him whisper her name.

Cabot Falls, Vermont
Present Day

Sofia's family filled the first two rows in the council hall. She noticed that Norton was not there. Matthew's presentation pointed out that the council defined *dwellings* as livable structures including all necessary utilities. He showed them plans of his tree house, showing that it was no more than the allowable child's playhouse. They removed the restriction and promised to reconsider lemonade stands at a later date.

The Parkers and McCrays celebrated with ice-cream cones, and after dropping Gina at the library, Sofia returned to the village records department. With her suspicions confirmed, she dialed Officer Quimby. "Did you know that all of the burned structures were for sale through Mark Keeler and insured through Keeler's wife? Although they show different insurers, she represents many different companies. She uses her maiden name, but it is strictly a family affair. The owners' names are fictitious. None of them exist—except Norton, of course." She told him what she had overheard in the parking garage.

"It's starting to make sense then," Officer Quimby told her. "I found out that Norton owned a furniture store in New Hampshire. He was suspected of burning it down to avoid bankruptcy. Darcie . . . uh, Inspector O'Leary and I think that Keeler knew about it and blackmailed him into the scheme here.

We're bringing Norton in for questioning. Maybe realizing that they were going to leave him to pay the piper will make Norton turn the tables on them."

"New Hampshire keeps turning up in the investigation. Why?" Sofia wanted to know.

"When I know, you'll know, Mrs. Parker. Meanwhile, I wouldn't worry about that lawsuit. I have a feeling that Norton will be too busy defending himself to continue that nonsense."

Buoyed by the news, Sofia stopped at the library to pick up Gina.

"Sofia, I can see why you love doing this research. I feel like a real detective too. And the mystery of Hannah Reed and Ann Johnson is solved. I found the terribly sad story of Allison Grey Johnson and the scoundrel she married. She was Hannah's mother, and she died just a few days after Hannah was born. The grandmother was too proud and had the baby anonymously placed in the orphanage. She later repented and left her fortune to Hannah Reed, whose birth name was Ann Johnson."

"Then that's why Hannah disappeared in 1872," Sofia said. "She used her real name."

"No, she didn't. She used the fortune, turning it into a home for needy women, and she married Zane Benetti, who I think must have been the Secret Service agent. I found the 1880 Vermont census that showed a Hannah Benetti married with four children—two boys and two girls, just like you, Sofia. She named the boys Zane and Vincent after her husband and her father-in-law. She named the girls Lily and Betsy. I guess we'll never know where the girls' names came from, but I like thinking of her sad life turning out so full of love."

Gina helped Sofia at La Dolce Vita over the successful Founder's Day celebration. Next door, a sign on the front door read A New U—Under New Management. The house next door to the Parkers had a For Sale sign posted in the front yard. Life had suddenly turned peaceful.

Officer Quimby and Inspector O'Leary stopped by the shop, holding hands. "Today we are just Ryan and Darcie," the young officer said. "I thought you'd want to know that Keeler and his banker friend, Watson, confessed to the fires. They planned to burn the entire row of downtown shops. The rest of the fires were so we wouldn't immediately suspect an insurance scam. Once the shops were destroyed, they thought that Cabot Trust would sell the property. It was an imperfect scheme conceived by Watson—whose real name is R. Cabot Grainger, a distant relative to the Cabots. He was angry that the Cabot estate was set up in a trust, and he couldn't get his hands on it."

"But why did they want to buy the property?" Sofia asked.

"He and Keeler had a cockamamy plan to turn Cabot Falls into a sort of resort with spa hotels where the shops are now and a sort of Disney park where the square is. We found the plans at his desk," Darcie said.

Ryan laughed. "As proof that he was a Cabot descendant, he produced documents he found among his mother's papers. Instead of helping him, they inadvertently proved that the original Cabot brother had incorporated the village, including all the land surrounding the inn. That ends the lawsuit between Cabot Falls and Grand Point."

"What about Norton?" Sofia asked.

"Keeler knew that Norton had burned down his furniture store in New Hampshire. He blackmailed Norton into taking part in the scheme. Grainger changed his name to Watson when he fled to Vermont shortly after Norton. That's how the Cabot Trust lost track of him," Ryan explained.

Darcie added, "We compared fingerprints gathered in New Hampshire to those we took from Watson here. They prove he's one and the same man."

"All three will be extradited to New Hampshire when we're through with them for arson," Ryan said. "Meanwhile, Norton hasn't stopped complaining, but now, it's about the jail food."

"Maybe I should take him a casserole," Sofia said. At the loud protests from her family, she laughed. "It was just a thought."

The truth was, Sofia was ready to put her cooking genes on hold. Her Hannah Reed gene was calling. She was ready to discover what other secrets the quilt held.

Learn more about Annie's fiction books at

AnniesFiction.com

- Access your e-books
- Discover exciting new series
- Read sample chapters
- Watch video book trailers
- Share your feedback

We've designed the Annie's Fiction website especially for you!

Plus, manage your account online!

- Check your account status
- Make payments online
- Update your address

Visit us at AnniesFiction.com